T0053734

AT BRIARWOOD SCHOOL *for* GIRLS

ALSO BY MICHAEL KNIGHT

Dogfight & Other Stories

Divining Rod

Goodnight, Nobody

The Holiday Season

The Typist

Eveningland

AT BRIARWOOD SCHOOL for GIRLS

A Novel

MICHAEL KNIGHT

Grove Press
New York

Published simultaneously in Canada
Printed in the United States of America

First Grove Atlantic edition: April 2019
First Grove Atlantic edition: April 2020

This book was set in 12.75-point Perpetua Std
by Alpha Design and Composition of Pittsfield, NH.

ISBN 978-0-8021-4892-6
eISBN 978-0-8021-4630-4

Library of Congress Cataloging-in-Publication data
is available for this title.

Grove Press
an imprint of Grove Atlantic
154 West 14th Street
New York, NY 10011

Distributed by Publishers Group West

groveatlantic.com

20 21 22 23 10 9 8 7 6 5 4 3 2 1

For Helen

AT BRIARWOOD SCHOOL for GIRLS

We have no obligation to make history. We have no obligation to make art. We have no obligation to make a statement. To make money is our only object.

—Michael Eisner, former CEO,
Walt Disney Company,
internal memo

JENNY: Are you a dream?
ELEANOR: I don't think so.
JENNY: Do you dream?
ELEANOR: I remember. That's like a dream.

—Eugenia Marsh, Act 1, Scene 3,
The Phantom of Thornton Hall

Question 1

In November of 1993, hoping to capitalize on the existing base for historical tourism in the area around Washington, DC, the Walt Disney Company announced its intention to build a theme park called Disney's America in rural Prince William County, Virginia. Which of the following was/were among the proposed attractions in the original plan?

A) A Native American encounter area, featuring a white-water rapids ride modeled on the journey of Lewis and Clark.

B) A turn-of-the-century steel town highlighted by a roller coaster that would plunge guests on a harrowing journey through a replica blast furnace.

C) A virtual-reality experience in which guests would be pursued by baying hounds and armed slave hunters during a thrilling Underground Railroad escape.

D) All of the above.

I

All boarding schools are haunted. Not infrequently by suicides. So it was at Briarwood School for Girls. According to campus lore, a young woman named Elizabeth Archer hanged herself with a bedsheet in Thornton Hall, her fiancé mustard-gassed at Belleau Wood, the thought of life without her love too much to bear. Ever since, residents had been reporting sudden drops in temperature, flickering lights. Actual sightings were rare but not unheard of. These brushes with the afterlife were easily debunked, attributable to drafty windows, touchy wiring, quirky ductwork, but there was a certain kind of Briarwood girl who longed to hear the creepy sounds at night, to behold a spirit, vague as mist, hovering through the wall.

It was not altogether remarkable, then, to come upon a group of students huddled around a Ouija board in the common room, candles reflected in the blank TV. On this occasion, Lenore Littlefield was outside looking in, hands cupped like parentheses beside her eyes, her breath fogging the window in the door. Poppy Tuttle and Melissa Chen pressed in close to peer over her shoulder. Lenore swiped condensation with the cuff of her peacoat, then mashed her nose against the glass again. She could see her roommate, Juliet Demarinis, and three other girls, bodies hunched over the board, hair hanging in their faces, shadows jumping in the candlelight. Lightly, doubtfully, Lenore rolled her fingertips against the pane. The dorms were locked at ten o'clock. After curfew, you were supposed to buzz the RA. The Ouija girls could have let them in without alerting anybody, but Juliet just smirked and waved.

"What the fuck?" Poppy said.

"I ate her Valentine's candy."

"Somebody sent Juliet Demarinis Valentine's candy?"

"Her dad. Italian truffles. I offered to buy her another box, but she said they had to be special ordered from Naples or someplace."

She'd been in bed listening to her Walkman to drown out her roommate's snoring. The scent of hazelnut heavy in the air. Her hunger was overwhelming, irresistible. She'd devoured the whole box. Even when she felt sick, Lenore was hungry all the time. She'd confessed first thing in the morning, and Juliet burst into tears.

"Let's just wait," Melissa said. "Somebody normal will come along."

Briarwood School for Girls was tucked away among old oaks and gentle hills between the towns of Haymarket and Manassas, a location that provided an abundance of field-trip opportunities and made for a picturesque brochure but offered next to nothing in the way of Friday night amusement for its boarders. Melissa, however, had a new black Jetta and a permission slip to drive off campus, so, after Lenore finished basketball practice, they'd cranked the radio and bolted, Poppy manning the music, Lenore stuck in the back, shuffling her feet among cassette cases and empty Slushee cups and leaning forward between the seats to keep up with the conversation. They'd stopped for beer at every convenience mart and country store for miles, but not one of them had a fake ID, and they'd failed to meet a sympathetic cashier or a man of legal age willing to make the purchase on their behalf. A wasted night, in other words, and in the end, at Poppy's insistence, they'd gone for fried-egg burgers at the Depot, and the waitress had taken forever with their check.

Poppy sat on the steps, scrounged a pack of Marlboro Lights from the pocket of her jeans, poked a wrinkled cigarette between her lips.

"Don't be stupid," Melissa said. "You'll get busted."

The cigarette twitched up and down as Poppy spoke. "In order for me to get busted, someone will have to open the door, and that's a good thing. It's bitter out here."

Thornton Hall leaked watery light over the grass, an illuminated boundary beyond which the rest of campus seemed far away, the pillars and arches, the modest slope of the grounds, the trees on the quad a tangle of black boughs. Lenore could close her eyes and picture Briarwood like a map, athletic fields and stables and a gatehouse down by the road, where the land was leveled off. Then the academic buildings, Murray Hall and Everett Hall and Brunson Hall and Ransom Library, all laid out around a quadrangle shaded with oaks and capped on one end by the Herndon Administration Annex and on the other by Hanover Chapel, its steeple silhouetted against the night. Above the quad, a little farther up the hill, were Burke Gymnasium and Beatrix Garvey Memorial Auditorium and then the dorms, Thornton and Blackford Halls, and Briarwood Manor, where Headmistress Mackey lived with her husband. At the very top of the hill, across a street called Shady Dell Loop, was Faculty Row, the houses one story, simple brick, painted white, most of them divided into duplexes. No moon tonight, or else it was hidden by smeary clouds. A bulb blinked on in the gatehouse, the security guard suddenly visible in its glow, hitching his pants, breathing into his hands. He'd be making his rounds before too long.

"Let me get one of those," Lenore said.

She sat beside Poppy on the steps, and Poppy shook a cigarette from the pack and passed the lighter to Lenore. Lenore took dainty drags, like sips.

"Do they really think they're talking to a ghost?" Melissa said.

The window in the door flickered like a jack-o'-lantern eye.

"They need to know," Poppy said, "if there are fat virgins on the other side."

Lenore said, "Have you ever done it, a Ouija board?"

"When I was like ten," Poppy said. "My neighbor's older sister had one, and we'd bring it out at slumber parties, ask about boys, stupid stuff. I'd move the thing around, mess with the other kids, answer their questions. But those girls, that's pathetic what's going on in there."

"Agreed," Melissa said, plopping down on Poppy's other side. She waved the smoke away, wrinkled her nose. "Your hair's gonna stink."

Poppy and Melissa were roommates. They had played Old Maid to sort it out. Whoever got caught with the queen of spades would find somebody else or take her chances in the lottery, but by the time Lenore started asking, everybody decent had paired up. They still shared a table in the dining hall and clumped together in their classes and drove around looking for trouble on Friday nights, but she couldn't shake the feeling that—what was it exactly that she felt? She had no intention of telling her friends about the weeks without her period, the pee tests to confirm. Now, Poppy tugged the scrunchie from her hair, gathered a blond handful, and reassembled her ponytail, cigarette tucked into the corner of her mouth.

"You know what really pisses me off?" she said.

But she never finished the thought. Before Lenore or Melissa could stop her, before they realized what she had in mind, she was on her feet and up the steps and at the door, thumbing the buzzer. Then she pressed it again. Lenore stubbed her cigarette out in a hurry and tossed the butt into the boxwoods, but Poppy just stood there until the RA appeared. Husna Hesbani was a senior. From Pakistan. Third in her class. She was wearing a Briarwood sweatshirt over her nightgown. Poppy made a show of plucking the cigarette from her lips and grinding it out under her shoe.

"Thank you, Husna. I hope we didn't interrupt your Friday night diddle."

Melissa picked up Poppy's butt and dropped it in the trash can by the door. "Do you have to write us up? Please, Husna. We're not that late."

Husna glanced at the clock. "Half an hour. That's late enough."

"You're a tyrant, Husna," Poppy said, "and no one likes you very much." Then she whirled to face the Ouija girls, ponytail sweeping the air. "Tell me, ladies, did the spirits advise you not to open the door?"

Juliet sat back on her heels. She looked pleased with her mischief, her eyes leering in the candlelight, a smear of zit cream on her chin.

"Does she sound drunk, Husna? I wonder if she's been drinking."

"What about it?" Husna said.

Poppy said, "I wish. What I am is bored. And sick of this place. I'm tired of stupid people and stupid fucking rules. I'm just tired, bitches, and I should probably go to bed."

With those words, she made her exit, both fists raised to give everyone the finger, Melissa scuttling after her down the hall. The Ouija girls returned their attention to the board, and Husna disappeared into her room, and candles threw trembling specters on the walls, and Lenore could imagine how her waking hours would play out—brushing her teeth and washing her face and slipping her headphones over her ears, hoping to fall asleep before Juliet came up, hoping, if she had been a certain kind of girl, for the gust across her skin, the hackles rising on her neck, a sad spirit crossing over from the next world into this.

II

Freshmen took turns ringing the old iron bell between classes and at mealtimes, one of those boarding-school traditions that had seemed quaintly exotic to Lucas Bishop when he'd first arrived at Briarwood. The bell was mounted at the center of the quad—thick rope dangling, clapper big as a fist. The sound of it carried from the gatehouse to Faculty Row. Bishop could hear it from the stoop outside his duplex, where he was nursing a second cup of coffee and studying the wet blanket of the sky, his Lab mix, Pickett, squatting in the yard next door. The bell rang exactly ten times, and by the final ring, girls were spilling from their dorms, headed to the dining hall for breakfast or to the library to finish up some homework before first period or to the parking lot to sneak a smoke. They were all hair and hands from that distance, the whole unruly flock of them veiled in puffs of winter breath. Today Bishop would chaperone his classes on their annual field trip to Manassas National Battlefield Park, and the sky did not bode well.

He whistled Pickett inside, then knotted his tie with shaky fingers, a trace of hangover behind his eyes. He washed three aspirin down with the cold dregs of his coffee. When he emerged, the sky seemed somehow closer to the ground.

The bus was waiting in the turnaround behind the Herndon Annex, the driver and Coach Fink hashing out the weather. At least two chaperones were required on all field trips. Bishop would not have chosen Coach Fink for her company, but she was willing, and her mornings were often free, and the students were afraid of her. She sported a Briarwood sweatsuit—green with white piping—over a turtleneck, one foot propped on the step of the bus, leg extended, body bent, nose touching her thigh. Her braid dangled almost to the pavement. If pressed, Bishop would have put her in her middle thirties, a daub of freckles lending a girlish aspect to her face. She was barely five foot three, but there was something aggressive about the way she took up space that made her appear taller than she was.

"Well," she said, "think it'll hold?"

"If we don't go today, then we're not going," Bishop said, and here came the bell again, and in no apparent hurry, students began to drift down from the quad, a stream of white blouses and plaid skirts, knee socks and saddle oxfords and peacoats, washing past Bishop and onto the bus. He called the roll, and Coach Fink paced the aisle taking a head count just in case. Fifty-eight junior girls. Coach Fink gave Bishop a thumbs-up, and Bishop told the driver they were ready, and off they went, the battlefield just a few miles up the road. He sat up front, behind the driver, while Coach Fink posted herself in back, where trouble was most likely to occur. It was too early in the year for such an outing, trees still leafless, pastures muddied by melted snow, the scene rolling by outside the windows nothing at all like what those doomed young men would have looked upon in July of 1861, but Bishop had to get through the Civil War, both world wars, and Vietnam before Briarwood released the girls for summer vacation.

Someone tapped him on the shoulder. Poppy Tuttle was sitting across the aisle and one row back, leaning toward him over her knees. "Do you like my button, Mr. Bishop?"

She thumbed the lapel of her peacoat forward so he could see the button more clearly—a silhouette of Mickey Mouse X-ed out over the letters *FTM*. She was also wearing long-johns bottoms under her skirt, both the button and the long johns violations of the dress code. Coach Fink could write Poppy up if she wanted to. Next to Poppy on the bench seat was Melissa Chen, and next to Melissa, by the window, was Lenore Littlefield. Lenore was asleep, it looked like, her mouth nodding open, her head on Melissa's shoulder.

"FTM?"

Poppy unfurled a smile. "Fuck the mouse," she said, and Bishop blinked three times. Slowly. Like a cat. Since Disney had announced its plans, there had been a bubbling of resistance and complaint but not enough, Bishop thought, to make a difference. The governor was on board with Disney, as were the chamber of commerce types. Money was already changing hands. Back in November, he had asked his students about Disney's America—How did they want the history of their country represented? Was there such a thing as historical authenticity, or were all portrayals of history corrupt in one way or another? Would Disney gloss over the darker elements of American history, and why was that important? But most of the girls seemed excited about the prospect of Mickey Mouse and the rest of the gang descending on Prince William County. Someone—Thessaly Roebuck? Marisol Brooks?—had even asked whether there might be future field trips to Disney's America in addition to or instead of the usual outings to Colonial Williamsburg and Monticello and Manassas National Battlefield Park. Poppy liked to raise the subject when she was bored as a way of distracting Bishop from the lesson. Just last week, she'd wondered how Disney would portray the Trail of Tears, and he'd let himself be suckered in, wasting half the class.

"Subtle," Bishop said.

"Poppy is nothing if not subtle," Melissa said, her voice low so as not to wake Lenore, but Lenore stirred anyway, lifting her head and wiping her mouth and looking around like she didn't know where she was.

The parking lot was mostly empty at this hour, wet leaves plastered to the pavement, the pavement dingy with road salt. Bishop left Coach Fink on the bus to keep an eye on the girls and headed inside the visitors' center. At the reception desk, he found a petition against Disney's America, and he signed it while he waited to meet the park ranger, a spry-looking elderly woman in a round-brimmed hat.

Their group numbered sixty, counting Bishop and Coach Fink, too many for such a tour, so many that the ranger had to shout to be heard at the back of the crowd, but this was a problem every year, and there was nothing to be done. Even shouting, some of what she said was lost to the wind. Bishop reassured himself that his students were well prepped. Two separate battles had been fought over this ground, both Confederate victories, the first announcing to the world that the American Civil War would be long and bloody and nothing at all like the glamorous military romp the politicians had imagined, the second paving the way for Robert E. Lee's push toward Antietam. His students would survive if the wind carried away a few lines of the ranger's script. Besides, the purpose of a field trip was not to gather information but to stand in the shadow of history, sift history through your fingers. Today, they would be focusing on the First Battle of Manassas. Bishop had been teaching at Briarwood for twelve years now. He'd been out there so many times he practically knew the script by heart. Next would come the bit about naïve government officials loading wagons with picnic supplies and hauling their families down from Washington to bear witness to a real battle.

"Obviously they were shocked by what transpired!" the ranger boomed.

Above a certain volume, the appropriate solemnity was impossible, and Bishop worried that his students would find the park ranger absurd. She led them past Henry House, where Judith Henry, the only civilian casualty of the battle, was killed in her bed by shrapnel from Union cannon fire, and along Matthews Hill, where the Confederate flank gave way. Coach Fink darted among the students like a sheepdog, nipping them silent with her glare. They lingered on the patch of hallowed ground where Stonewall Jackson rallied the nearly whipped Confederates, earning his nickname and his reputation and a monument in his honor—Jackson in the saddle, fist propped on his hip, both man and horse as overmuscled as comic-book superheroes. "I'll never cease to be amazed," the ranger bellowed, "at the depth of human courage." Poppy Tuttle and Lenore Littlefield and Melissa Chen were milling along at the back of the crowd, Bishop close enough to hear that they were talking but too far behind to make out what they said.

"Not interested?"

Poppy flipped her ponytail out from under the collar of her coat.

"Quite the contrary, Mr. Bishop. We were just debating what to bring on a picnic to a battle. I said beer and burgers like at a tailgate party."

"But if you brought burgers you'd have to cook them," Melissa said, "and how would you keep the beer cold? That all sounds like more trouble than it's worth."

Lenore said, "Did they even have beer in the Civil War?"

"Definitely they had beer," Poppy said. "The Sumerians invented beer."

"You would know that," Melissa said.

Bishop understood that they had been talking about no such thing when he interrupted, and he was amazed, as he often was, by the quickness of their minds. Ask a Briarwood girl to walk you through the Bill of Rights and who knows what kind of answer you might get, but catch her chatting on a field trip and here's a plausible comedic riff on battlefield picnics and the history of beer. Bishop was forty-two years old, the son of a parole officer and a librarian. He would have been terrified of girls like these when he was their age.

"It must seem crazy to you," he said, "but think about Desert Storm. I know I was sitting on my couch with a bag of chips watching night-vision images of bombs obliterating Baghdad. I'll bet you were, too. At least your parents were. History's a stickler for repeating itself."

"That's not exactly the same thing," Melissa said.

"It's the same impulse. The war probably didn't seem real to those people. That footage from Iraq sure didn't."

"The question," Poppy said, "is, did they have chips in the Civil War?"

Bishop did his good-sport smile.

"They had chips," he said, "and they had beer."

The tour was moving again, the ranger waving everyone along, the sky looming low over the trees. Bishop gazed off toward the road, the visitors' center. He loved that story about the picnicking Washington dignitaries, their wagons gumming up the Union retreat. He had always been intrigued by the oddball details of history, by the extras as much as the stars. Along the front, facing the parking lot, the visitors' center was outfitted with a colonnade, giving it a veneer of the antique, but from this side, it looked as redbrick institutional as a rest stop off the interstate.

"Where'd you get that button?" Bishop said.

Poppy dipped her chin to look, like she'd forgotten it was there. She unclipped the pin, slipped it through Bishop's lapel, fixed the clasp. She patted his chest with the flat of her hand.

"Fuck the mouse," she said.

Lenore rolled her eyes and stifled a yawn.

"Have you been to Disney World, Mr. Bishop?"

"As a matter of fact, no. I was already in college when it opened."

"It's not so bad," she said.

Coach Fink was standing like a fence post beside the trail. Arms crossed in her sweatsuit. Waiting. The girls dropped into single file as they passed. Today was Monday. By Wednesday, Bishop's classes would be finished with the Civil War and through the Reconstruction. Thursday, review. Test on Friday. Then on to a new century and World War I.

As Bishop drew abreast, Coach Fink said, "I could hear you jawing from thirty yards."

Bishop touched the button on his lapel. "History lesson," he said, and at just that moment, the bottom fell out of the sky. The tour dissolved in a mad dash for the visitors' center. The students took off at a sprint, and Coach Fink took off in hot pursuit, but Bishop lingered there, rain running in his ears and down his neck and beating on the battlefield all around him.

III

In the senior section of the 1976 edition of *The Green and White* hides a photograph of young Patricia Fink, Coach Fink nowadays to her players and her peers, though her classmates had called her Tricia. In this photograph, young Coach Fink is smiling beneath Farrah Fawcett bangs, her round face freckled and open and unlined, her nose upturned, her blue eyes optimistic and unperturbed, her teeth sheathed in a delicate tangle of braces. Deeper into the yearbook, all the way back in Activities and Athletics, are several more images of young Coach Fink—driving hard to the basketball hoop against archrival Saint Mary's of the Green, swatting a field hockey ball during a sideline hit. The image, however, that would have startled her players and her peers, had they stumbled across it, features young Coach Fink in a white nightgown and a dark wig, barely recognizable, freckles blanked with stage makeup, hand in hand with a young man from Woodmont School, the two of them singing "Somewhere" from *West Side Story*, in which she'd played Maria, a stretch to be sure, considering her appearance, but her voice had been too beautiful to give the role to someone else.

Even today, on this Tuesday evening, making her way from basketball practice to Beatrix Garvey Memorial Auditorium, she could remember most of the lyrics to most of the songs, and she could remember the young man's name—Wilson Barber, as Tony—and how his palms went clammy when he held her hands and the way he squinted because the director refused to let him wear his glasses. This day would be her first as faculty adviser to the Drama Club. Her predecessor, Margaret Rowan, had taken leave to care for her ailing mother back in Baltimore. Ms. Rowan also taught American Lit. Her classes had been handed over to Lucille Pinn, the riding instructor, who, it turned out, had majored in English at Bryn Mawr. Headmistress Mackey had been ensconced at Briarwood for more than thirty years, and she had not forgotten Coach Fink's performance in *West Side Story*. It was determined that this arrangement would suffice until end of term, when either Ms. Rowan's mother would have passed or a permanent replacement could be found.

Now, Coach Fink shouldered through the double doors and crossed the lobby on the balls of her feet and then through another set of doors into the auditorium proper. There, standing on the lip of the stage, waving a sheaf of papers like she was in charge, was a student Coach Fink recognized but could not name. Degrassi? Debussey? Plump, pale. Definitely not an athlete. Half a dozen other students slouched in the first few rows. Coach Fink took the proscenium steps two at a time.

"Who are you supposed to be?" she said to the girl who was definitely not an athlete.

"Juliet. Juliet Demarinis."

"Park it, Demarinis," Coach Fink said.

She waited for the girl to be seated, then linked her hands behind her back and began to pace, words coming to her in rhythm with her steps.

"We're all sorry about Ms. Rowan's mother, but I know, if she was here, she would tell us to knuckle down and make her proud. There are things in life we can't control, and that's too bad, but one thing we can control is how we rise to this occasion." Her sneakers squeaked when she pivoted on the stage. "The first thing we have to do is decide on a production." A hand shot up among the students, but Coach Fink ignored it. "I was thinking *West Side Story*. It's a classic, and I'm—" The hand in the air was frantic now, the waving accompanied by a peeping sound. Coach Fink glared to let the waver know that such intrusions would not be tolerated, but the girl did not desist.

"What is it, Debussey?"

"Demarinis," the waver said. "It's just that—"

"Let me ask you a question, Demarinis. Do you interrupt Ms. Sharp or Mr. Bishop in the middle of their lectures?"

"No, ma'am."

"Do you interrupt your mother when she's trying to tell you something? Do you interrupt your pastor during a sermon?"

"No, but—"

"Then what makes you think it's acceptable to wave your hand at me and make animal noises when I'm giving a pep talk?"

"I'm sorry, Coach Fink. It's just, we've already decided on a production. Ms. Rowan chose *The Phantom of Thornton Hall*."

She held up the sheaf of papers again, a script. "This year is the twentieth anniversary of the first Broadway performance, but it's never been done on campus."

This information stopped Coach Fink. *The Phantom of Thornton Hall* had been written by one of Briarwood's most famous graduates: Eugenia Marsh, class of '62, winner of the Pulitzer Prize. The play remained required reading in American Lit, but because it was set on the campus of a boarding school very much like Briarwood, and because it dealt with sensitive subject matter—teen pregnancy, suicide—the administration had traditionally frowned on its performance. That was not the kind of thing parents and potential donors wanted to see. Coach Fink squeezed her hands into fists, released them, balled her fingers tight again.

"Not a musical?" she said.

"No, ma'am."

"Has Headmistress Mackey signed off on this?"

"Yes, ma'am."

"Then why didn't she say anything to me?"

"I don't know, ma'am."

Coach Fink pointed at a redhead sipping from a can of Sprite.

"You—what's your name?"

The girl mumbled a reply.

"Speak up," Coach Fink said. "You sound like you've got a mouthful of mashed potatoes."

"Thessaly Roebuck."

"Let me ask you something, Roebuck. Is Demarinis here a good egg?"

"What—egg? I don't understand."

"I want to know if what Demarinis says is true, or if she's the kind of sorry human being to pull a fast one on a newly appointed faculty adviser to the Drama Club."

"You can ask Headmistress Mackey yourself," Demarinis said.

Her best option, Coach Fink thought, was probably just to turn the whole business over to Demarinis and let the Drama Club get on with whatever they had planned, but ceding authority wasn't Coach Fink's MO, and she felt the strongest urge to make Demarinis drop and give her twenty. Beyond the basic subject matter, the particulars of *The Phantom of Thornton Hall*, like the particulars of "A Diamond as Big as the Ritz" and "A Good Man Is Hard to Find," of "After Apple-Picking" and "I heard a Fly buzz – when I died," had washed over Coach Fink without making much impression, just enough to earn her reliable C, and then on out to the field hockey pitch or into the echoey gym, where she could lose herself, become herself, where she understood the nature of the world, where it didn't matter that she remained undiscovered by the boys at Woodmont or Prince William Military Academy or that certain girls made certain jokes at her expense, misguided, unimaginative jokes reserved for the kind of young women who preferred field hockey and basketball to dressage and winter formals.

The doors from the lobby clattered, and everyone turned to look. Lenore Littlefield appeared at the top of the aisle.

"Littlefield?" Coach Fink said. "You need something?"

"I'm here for the Drama Club meeting."

Littlefield was Coach Fink's swingman, not her best player by a long shot, but she showed flashes of toughness and speed, and Coach Fink had never been more pleased to see her.

"I didn't know you were in the Drama Club."

Demarinis blurted, "That's because she's not."

"I missed curfew last weekend," Littlefield said. "Headmistress Mackey told me I could earn off the demerits with an extracurricular. She said the Drama Club needed bodies for the spring show."

Coach Fink's first impulse was to berate the girl for missing curfew—bonehead infractions like that could get her suspended from the team—but she was buoyed by the possibility of an ally, and she sensed a familiar fluctuation in the air, a shift in momentum. She knew from experience that there were moments and decisions in every contest that seemed insignificant as they occurred but that ultimately shaped the outcome. Sometimes, if you were paying attention, those moments could be detected before the crucial decision had been made. At times like that, life slowed down and Coach Fink's vision went sharp, the edges of everything perfectly defined.

Demarinis slapped her script against her knees. "We don't need anybody. There are only five speaking parts, and Ms. Rowan already—"

"Button it, Debussey," Coach Fink said.

Question 2

In 1979, after the critical and commercial failure of her second play, *Dream Entropy*, Eugenia Marsh gave up writing, abandoned the limelight of Broadway, and refused all media inquiries. To which of the following locations did she retreat?

A) A cottage in the Five Islands area on the southern coast of Maine.

B) A farmhouse in the foothills of the Blue Ridge Mountains of Virginia.

C) A log cabin in Idaho's Salmon River valley.

D) An artists' commune in the desert outside Santa Fe.

IV

Trailing archrival Saint Mary's of the Green 36–34, with nineteen seconds on the clock, Bunny English deflected a pass midair, rerouting the flight of the ball directly into the hands of Rachel Milner. Rachel zipped the ball to point guard Veronica Tuck, who was already moving into fast-break position, and Veronica bounce-passed to Lenore Littlefield, who was sprinting ahead on the wing. In the time it took to dribble once, twice, several alternatives presented themselves to Lenore, all of which she processed, thanks to hours of drills and repetition, without having to think about them much at all: she could pass the ball back to Veronica, thus bringing the fast break to a halt and allowing the defense into position; she could pull up for a fifteen-foot jumper, a low-percentage shot; or she could attempt a risky pass across the defense to power forward Brunhilde Shimmel, who was streaking into the paint from the opposite side of the court. In that next moment, as the ball was rising for the third time toward her palm, before a decision had been made, when all her options remained equally viable, Lenore's vision fuzzed, and her head felt suddenly a long way from her feet, and the thrum of the crowd receded like someone was twisting a knob—the gym, the school, the whole world of possibilities dissolving into nothing.

She came to on her back with a ring of faces hovering over her, each face a ring of its own, and in each face two more rings of worried eyes. Gradually, the nearest of those faces resolved into Coach Fink, the heat in her cheeks highlighting her freckles. "Give her some air," she was shouting. "Everybody back off, back off," but none of the other faces withdrew.

"Can you hear me?" she said in a smaller voice. "Littlefield, you with us?"

Lenore felt herself nodding, though she was not aware of instructing her head to move.

Coach Fink swung a glare around the ring. "Back off now. I said give her room, ladies. Let her breathe," and this time the faces disappeared from view, leaving only Coach Fink, her hand tucked under Lenore's head, the hot white lights in the ceiling burning like distant stars.

"Did we win?" Lenore said.

A spasm passed across Coach Fink's eyes and mouth like someone had given her a pinch. She looked away and told someone to elevate Lenore's legs, and Lenore felt her feet rising from the floor.

"How many fingers am I holding up?" Coach Fink said.

"Three."

"How many now?"

"Still three."

"You're OK. I don't think you hit your head."

"Did we win?" Lenore asked again.

"The ball went out of bounds. Saint Mary's possession."

"That's not good," Lenore said.

"Let's see if we can't get you to the bench."

A smattering of applause broke out among the players on the court and the couple of dozen spectators in the bleachers as Coach Fink helped Lenore to her feet. She hardly noticed Coach Fink handing her off to the team doctor, Brunhilde Shimmel's grandfather, a retired podiatrist who lived nearby and never missed a home game. He flicked his penlight across her pupils, patted her knee, then turned away to watch Saint Mary's kill the clock.

Lenore was in bed reading *The Phantom of Thornton Hall*, 10,000 Maniacs jangling in her Walkman, when Coach Fink rapped on the door and pushed it open without waiting for a reply.

"How do you feel?"

Lenore pulled the headphones down around her neck.

"Fine," she said.

Coach Fink picked up a can of Diet Coke on the nightstand and glared at the label like she'd caught Lenore red-handed drinking beer.

"This stuff will eat a hole in your stomach."

She disappeared into the hall, still carrying the can, and Lenore returned her attention to the script. The play concerned a boarding-school student named Jenny March—pregnant, scared, confused—who is visited one winter night by the ghost of Eleanor Bowman. Lenore liked how Jenny hardly talked about how she was pregnant and Eleanor never talked about her suicide. They mostly just talked about little things, regular things. Eleanor's ghost is creepy and sad, but eventually Jenny begins to take a kind of comfort in her presence. Lenore had been assigned the role of Bridget, Jenny's roommate. Bridget didn't have too many lines.

When Coach Fink reappeared, she was holding a paper cup.

"Drink this," she said.

"Now?"

"I want to watch you drink it. You probably just got dehydrated."

Lenore forced the water down, dribbling on her chin. She wiped her mouth on her shoulder.

"I'm sorry, Coach," she said. "I wish I hadn't fainted."

Coach Fink's eyes dropped to the pages in Lenore's lap.

"Ah, screw it," she said.

She retrieved the cup from Lenore, crushed it into a ball, and with a flick of her wrist sent it spinning into the trash can by the door.

"Let me ask you something, Littlefield. How do you think the play is looking so far? You think rehearsals are going OK?"

"I guess so."

"Bull dook. We look like hell. There's something wrong with the lineup, but I can't figure what it is." Coach Fink made a bitter face, as if she didn't like the taste of what she'd just said. "Where's your roommate?"

Lenore glanced at Juliet's bed, neatly made, a stuffed lamb propped on the pillow, so old and well loved its fur was nearly worn away.

"Watching TV, I think. In the common room."

Coach Fink disappeared again, and Lenore lifted the headphones into place and let her eyes fall on the script. There were moments when all the things Jenny and Eleanor weren't talking about caught her breath up in her throat. She set the script aside and clicked her Walkman off and replaced 10,000 Maniacs with the Cure. A minute later, Coach Fink returned, hauling Juliet Demarinis by the wrist.

"Do you know what happened at the game tonight?"

"I have no idea," Juliet said.

"Why am I not surprised?" Coach Fink said. "I'll tell you what happened. Your roommate passed out during a fast break. I want you to stay here and keep an eye on her. If she acts funny, you come and get me. I'm up on Faculty Row, third house from the end. Clear?"

"Not even a little."

Lenore heard their exchange beneath the music, gestures and expressions more pronounced than words.

Juliet kept her alarm clock on the bureau across the room so she'd have to get out of bed in the morning to shut it off, one of many habits that had gotten under Lenore's skin. The numbers on the clock flipped like a Rolodex when the time changed, the clock humming for an instant just before the change, as if gathering itself, as if advancing the time required tremendous effort, then rattling as the new minute or hour rolled into place, the sound itself as much a part of Lenore's irritation as the position of the clock, and though she couldn't actually hear it, because of the headphones, knowing it was making the sound was almost as annoying as the sound itself. She watched it now, that clock, watched the minutes roll past. Neither Lenore nor Juliet spoke, each in her separate bed.

They didn't have anything in common. That was the problem. Juliet was from Albany, Lenore from Charleston. Juliet's parents had been married forever; Lenore's parents had been divorced since she was eight. Juliet's dad worked at a textile plant; Lenore's dad worked in a bank. Juliet's mom sold cosmetics out of her car; Lenore's mom lunched with her friends. Juliet was a scholarship kid; Lenore's mother and her mother's mother were steadfast Briarwood girls. Juliet liked Snapple and overalls and Drama Club and Emily Dickinson and Rollerblades and flavored popcorn and stuffed animals, and Lenore liked none of those things. Now Lenore was stuck with Drama Club, and Poppy and Melissa had thirty hours of school service, akin to community service, except that it usually involved some chore like shelving books in the library—one reason it was so hard to find anything in the library when you needed it. On top of all that, because of the cigarette, Poppy was on campus restriction until the end of the year.

Lenore shut off the music and looked at Juliet.

"You don't have to hang around," she said.

"Yes," Juliet said, "I do."

"I won't tell Coach Fink."

Juliet swiveled around so that her body was perpendicular to the mattress, facing Lenore. "You know she's ruining the play. The first time in history *The Phantom of Thornton Hall* has been performed at Briarwood, and it's going to be a disaster thanks to her."

Lenore didn't like hearing her coach demeaned, not by Juliet Demarinis anyway, but it was hard to argue with what she'd said. Most of the cast were so intimidated by Coach Fink that they delivered their lines as if reading ransom notes at gunpoint. Juliet was playing Eleanor.

"She asked me tonight how I thought rehearsals were going."

"What'd you say?"

"I told her they were fine, but she thinks there's something wrong with the lineup."

"The lineup? Did she mean the cast? Does she plan to make a change?"

Lenore shrugged, savoring her roommate's panic.

"Oh God," Juliet said, bolting to her feet, arms stiff at her sides. "She hates me. She'll give Eleanor to someone else. You're her favorite. She'll probably give the part to you."

Now it was Lenore's turn to be worried. She hadn't considered that. Eleanor was one of the leads. Juliet bugged her eyes and snapped her fingers, inspiration striking so visibly a lightbulb might have popped into being over her head. She knelt on the floor and reached under her bed, emerging with a long, flat cardboard box.

"We'll ask the Ouija board," she said.

"You're kidding."

"Do not mock that which you do not understand."

"I have a hard time believing that anything sold at Kmart has magical powers."

Juliet set the board on the floor between their beds. "The board doesn't have magical powers. It's just a conduit. Now get down here. I can't do this by myself."

The board was faux wood grain, with the letters of the alphabet marked in two arches as if branded into the wood. Beneath the letters was a row of numbers, 0 to 9, and beneath the numbers the words *Good Bye*. In the top right-hand corner, Lenore saw a crescent moon and the word *no*; in the top left, *yes* and a sun.

Juliet said, "Get the overhead, please. And light that candle on my dresser before you sit."

Lenore did as her roommate asked, using a book of matches by the candle. When she hit the switch, the effect was less a loss of light than as if all light in the room had concentrated in the flame. She sat cross-legged like Juliet. Juliet scooched forward so their knees were touching. When they made contact, Lenore felt something like static passing between them, but it was only the prick of stubble on Juliet's legs. She resisted the urge to flinch, to tease. She had to admit she was intrigued.

Juliet balanced the board across their knees and held up a triangle-shaped wedge about the size of her hand. Through a hole in the center of the wedge, Lenore could see Juliet's lips moving as she spoke.

"This is called the planchette. If you've ever seen a horror movie then you know basically how it works."

She set the planchette on the board, the hole centered over the letter *G*, and instructed Lenore to touch it very lightly with her index and middle fingers.

"You have to be respectful. Empty your thoughts and focus on the planchette. If you can't be serious, the spirits won't speak."

"I'll try," Lenore said. "I'm a little nervous."

Juliet smiled at Lenore, a real smile, then shut her eyes. She drew in a deep breath and held it a moment before exhaling.

"Oh spirits," she said, "we bring you greetings and good wishes from the living world. We do not wish to disturb your rest. We humbly ask for your help. Are you there, spirits? How many spirits are in this room?"

The planchette didn't budge. Juliet's breath whistled in her nose.

"Are you there, spirits?" she said again. "We beseech you to make your presence known."

This time, Lenore felt the planchette move under her fingers. She watched, heart pounding, as it made its way slowly, haltingly, up and to the right, until it settled over the moon.

"You're doing that," she said.

Juliet screwed up her face. "The moon means we're in contact with a good spirit. Show some respect." She straightened and relaxed her face again. "Oh spirit," she said. "We thank you for revealing your presence on this night. My name is Juliet Demarinis. With me is Lenore Littlefield. We come to you with matters of concern to us both. What is your name, good spirit?"

The planchette didn't move. If Juliet was faking, Lenore thought, she had her routine down pat. She had the undeniable sense that someone was listening. Juliet tried again.

"Is this the spirit of Elizabeth Archer?"

The planchette jerked suddenly to the left, stopping over *yes*.

Lenore whispered, "Holy shit," and Juliet wagged her eyebrows.

"Thank you, Elizabeth. It is a pleasure to be in your company again. Might we trouble you with a question?"

The planchette skidded in a wide arc left and down and up again to *yes*. Lenore was sure of one thing: she wasn't moving it.

Juliet said, "We wish to know if Coach Fink—" but Lenore cut her off.

"Wait," she said.

"What?"

"I don't know. It just seems like, if this is real, I mean, doesn't it seem a little silly to ask about the play?"

"It's not silly. The play's about her life. You know Eleanor is based on Elizabeth Archer, right?"

"I guess," Lenore said, "but still."

"Well, what do you want to ask about?"

Lenore could imagine a hundred questions, just none she was willing to ask in front of Juliet. Before she could think of anything, the planchette began to move. Down and left to *B*. Left again to *A*. Then a slow loop over the board before returning to *B*.

"Is that you?" Juliet said. "You better not be screwing around."

Lenore shook her head. She couldn't speak. The planchette inched to the right and drifted down, and Lenore jerked her hands away before it reached the letter *Y*. She scrambled backward onto her bed, upsetting the board, the planchette clattering under the nightstand.

"What are you doing?" Juliet said. "She's trying to send us a message."

Lenore said, "No fucking way," and even after the lights were on, the board returned to its box, the box stowed out of sight, Lenore refused to tell her roommate what had spooked her.

V

Bishop avoided the dining hall on Saturday mornings because the girls tended to show up for breakfast in their pajamas. They didn't seem to mind his presence, but he felt like he was witnessing something private. Instead, he fired up his old Subaru and hung a left after the gatehouse, his dog riding shotgun, his view split by a crack jagging from his inspection sticker down to the windshield wiper on the opposite side. They passed farmhouses with vinyl siding. They passed the place that called itself an antique market but sold mostly junk, novelty ashtrays and colored-glass bottles and board games in tattered boxes. They passed a hair salon in somebody's garage. They passed three churches. Drive an hour in any direction and you ran across the boom and sprawl of DC bedroom communities or old plantations bought up by movie stars and tycoons, but Bishop knew that history had been less kind to this part of the state.

Briarwood School for Girls had been founded in 1868 by the Reverend E. Rex Hanover on the estate of his friend and benefactor, the widow Charlotte Brunson, who had lost her husband and her three sons in the Civil War. Those original students received instruction on the first floor of Briarwood Manor, one of only a handful of structures in the vicinity spared the torch when Union troops passed through after Second Manassas. Widow Brunson had earned a reprieve by allowing her home to be used as a hospital. Most everything else in the town of Haymarket had been burned to cinder, every house and every stable, every business and every barn, as the Yankees hobbled back toward Washington.

They passed a gas station advertising lottery tickets for sale and videos for rent. They passed the new McDonald's and the old Dairy Queen. They rolled into Manassas—the barbershop, the florist, the funeral home, the Depot Diner. Bishop parked between a sheriff's cruiser and a custom van with a mermaid painted on the panel, long wet hair covering her breasts. He left Pickett in the car with the window cracked, bought a copy of the *Washington Post* from the machine outside the door, and took a booth beside the window. The waitress, Regina, was chatting up a pair of sheriff's deputies.

"Y'all ever catch those boys," she was saying, "that sprayed graffiti on the high school?"

"'Fraid not."

"I wonder sometimes what y'all do over there. Do you even bother with police work or do you just come in here to bother me?"

They laughed and blushed and dropped their eyes, and Regina bumped one of the deputies with her hip. She turned smoothly on her heel, eyes blank for a moment, glazed and bored, then flickering alive again as she scooped a menu from the rack and crossed to Bishop's booth.

"Hey, sweetie. Cup of coffee?"

"And orange juice, please," Bishop said.

He watched her move around behind the counter to fill his drinks, her demeanor so blatantly carnal it seemed almost a put-on. The dye job, the short skirt, the tan and freckled cleavage. Her nose was large and hooked, a feature that would have overwhelmed the faces of most women but that somehow, like the figurehead on the prow of a ship, accentuated her allure.

In the last decade, Bishop had had exactly two romantic relationships, both short-lived, the first with Debbie Wicker, a real estate agent in Manassas, the second with a former colleague, an algebra teacher named Rebecca Flood. He broke it off with Debbie when it became clear she wanted him to marry her, and Rebecca ended things with him when she decided to go back to grad school for her PhD. Neither had lasted longer than ten months. Both had ended amicably enough. He hadn't heard from Rebecca since she left, but he still sometimes bumped into Debbie, married now, mother of two, and she treated him with fond pity, like a screwup younger brother who had plenty of potential but couldn't get his act together. They'd met when Bishop had briefly considered buying a house of his own, and whenever they crossed paths, she mentioned a listing or two she thought he might like, but his ambitions toward ownership had faded.

When Regina returned, he said, "Is that your van?"

She cracked a smile, exposing the gap between her teeth. "You like it? My ex gave it up instead of alimony. I like it all right, but I'm still not sure it suits me."

Bishop didn't know what to say to that. He ordered pancakes and bacon in lieu of a reply. Regina left to carry his ticket to the kitchen, and he opened his newspaper—an article about Aldrich Ames, who'd sold state secrets to the Soviets, another about Nancy Kerrigan and Tonya Harding. He wasn't interested. In the bottom right-hand corner of page three, however, he found an article headlined *Reclusive Playwright Breaks Silence to Denounce Theme Park*. Apparently, Eugenia Marsh had dashed off an angry letter to the editor, but her star had dimmed enough that it took the staff some time to make the connection between letter-writing crank and winner of the Pulitzer Prize. Now, they were running with the personal angle. There were excerpts from her letter—*If we are defined by our past, doesn't it follow that Disney's synthetic version of history threatens our understanding of what it means to be human?*—but it was not reprinted in full. Of greater interest were Marsh's long silence and the rumors that she had spent time in a mental institution following the failure of her second play, juicy sidebar material to spice up an otherwise dry debate. Disney CEO Michael Eisner was unavailable for comment, but his media-relations team had issued a statement:

> We are disappointed by Ms. Marsh's letter but not entirely surprised. Her personal issues are well documented and her unfounded statements situate her among the intellectual elitists who don't seem to care about the thousands of regular people who will benefit from this project. Governor Allen, along with former Governor Wilder and dozens of local business leaders, recognize

> that Disney's America will allow guests to celebrate the diversity of this great nation and to explore the conflicts that have defined our character in a way that is respectful to the past and to the region, while creating sorely needed jobs and investing in necessary infrastructure.

They'd printed a photo with the piece, an old professional head shot by the looks of it, Eugenia Marsh twenty years ago, with her chin propped in her right hand, a cigarette between her fingers, hair clipped into a bob.

"I'll be damned," he said out loud, just as Regina was swinging over with his food.

"What for?"

He told her about the letter, the article. "Eugenia Marsh hasn't spoken to the press in fifteen years."

"Eugenia who?"

"She's a playwright. Or she was. She went to Briarwood. She won the Pulitzer Prize back in the seventies."

Regina set his plate on the table and refilled his coffee from a pot. She huffed the bangs out of her eyes.

"You work up there, right?"

"I teach history."

He could almost see the curiosity draining out of her.

"Let me ask you something," Bishop said, delaying her a moment longer. "What do you think about this Disney stuff? You think it's a good idea?"

Regina shrugged and switched the pot to her other hand.

"Once the park is up and running, maybe this place will do enough business that I won't have to drive my ex's custom van."

Bishop poured syrup on his pancakes and stared at the photograph of Eugenia Marsh. He stared long enough to register the small details—the pearl cuff links in her shirt, the tortoiseshell cigarette holder, the way the heel of her hand mashed faint dimples into her chin.

After a while, Regina returned with his check.

"That your dog?" she said, pointing.

Pickett had moved over into the driver's seat. He was resting one paw on the wheel like he was steering, his expression serious, his gaze focused through the window on Bishop in his booth. The image was charming, the kind of thing you might find on a greeting card.

"That's him."

"I wonder where he thinks he's going," Regina said.

They passed the train station and crossed the tracks, the heater slow to warm the car. Bishop had been out to the Disney site once before, not long after the announcement. He'd just wanted to see it, he supposed, wanted to know what would be lost. Pickett whined and scratched the window, and Bishop said, "It's too cold, buddy. You want some music? How about a little music?" He turned on the radio, spun the dial—religion, sports, country, top 40, religion, top 40, talk, country, sports—then turned it off. His cassette player was busted, a French-language instructional tape jammed in its gears, left over from a time when he had plotted a course toward self-improvement. He'd quit drinking on weeknights. Bought a pair of hand weights, did curls and overhead presses while watching TV. The French was meant to broaden his horizons, but when the cassette player broke, the rest of the plan fell by the wayside.

He kept driving until woods pressed in along the road, beer cans and fast-food bags littering the drainage ditches. When he spotted surveyor's tape banded to the trunks of occasional trees, he pulled onto the shoulder, cut the engine. Pickett turned an excited circle in his seat.

"Hold your horses," Bishop said.

He stepped out and checked the road for traffic before turning Pickett loose. The dog sprinted in a wide arc, running the kinks out. They set off into the woods, moving in a straight line from the car, no destination in mind. Pickett trotted up with a branch in his mouth, too big for throwing, so Bishop broke it on his knee and launched a piece as far as he could. Pickett brought it back a moment later, and Bishop wondered at the aptitude required to locate a particular fallen branch in a universe of fallen branches. He'd read that Disney had bought these woods from Exxon, more than two thousand acres of them, though he had no idea what an oil company would be doing in possession of undeveloped woods in this part of Virginia. He had to admit the site was perfect. This was not old growth. The land had once been cleared, then let go to seed, spindly oaks and pines creeping back in over whatever had been here before. Nobody would care much when they were cut. Most people would be happy for the work. He stopped and looked around, tried to imagine the swarms of tourists, the midways and the rides, a Technicolor simulacrum of American history. He thought of Eugenia Marsh breaking her long silence to write that letter. Some things were worth preserving. He believed that. So what was the harm in dressing the history up a little, making it shine, remembering the good more than the bad?

He turned and walked back the way they'd come, chucking the branch for Pickett again and again until they reached the road. They emerged a few hundred yards from the car, and Bishop patted his hip, setting the dog to heel. As they drew closer, he saw a man peering into the window of the Subaru. He noted the uniform, the idling cruiser.

He called hello, and the deputy hooked his thumbs into his belt. Bishop recognized him from the diner. His partner was in the cruiser, mouthing into the radio.

"This is my car," Bishop said. "Is there a problem?"

"You can't park here."

"I'm sorry, Officer. I just wanted to look around."

"You're lucky I haven't already had you towed. Also, that dog is not on a leash. There are ordinances in this county."

"We'll just get out of your way," Bishop said.

He opened the door, and Picket hopped into the back seat.

"Easy now," the deputy said, tensing as if he thought Bishop was about to make a run for it. "I need to see your license and registration."

Bishop protested, but the deputy would not be moved, so he produced the documents and waited in the car while the deputy conferred with his partner. Pickett curled up with his tail over his nose. After a few minutes, the deputy returned with a pair of citations, one for illegal parking, the other for walking Pickett without a leash. He explained how Bishop could pay the fines if he wished to avoid a court appearance. Then he rested his forearms on the door and gave Bishop a hard look.

"Do I know you?" he said.

"I saw you at the Depot. I was just there."

The deputy shook his head.

"I don't think that's it," he said.

He banged on the roof, twice, with the flat of his hand, making Pickett jump up and look around, tail slapping the seats. Bishop watched him walk away in the rearview mirror. For what seemed like a long time, the two cars sat there idling on the shoulder. Bishop didn't want to be the first to leave, but the cruiser flicked its headlights, so he dropped the Subaru into gear and motored off, shadows brushing down through the trees.

VI

For more than a week now, Coach Fink had been plagued by versions of the same bad dream. It wasn't a nightmare exactly, but it woke her breathless and disoriented and left her groggy for the rest of the day. In these dreams she was waiting for a letter, sometimes here at Briarwood but more often in a small clapboard house at the end of a gravel lane. The land around the house was worn out and dusty, a cornfield recently harvested. She'd never seen this house before. She walked from the porch to the mailbox at the end of the lane, back and forth and back and forth, but the letter never came.

The dream would not have troubled her but for the side effects. Coach Fink had always been an avid dreamer, especially around times of significant real-life events. Back in school, for example, on the nights before a game, she'd often dreamed that she was having sex with someone famous—Sean Connery or Clint Eastwood, usually, but once with Raquel Welch. Before an exam, she sometimes dreamed she was in a canoe rushing toward a waterfall or that her hair was on fire and she couldn't put it out. Grogginess, however, she could not abide. She had no time for grogginess.

She decided to raise the subject with the riding instructor, Lucille Pinn. Lucille was the nearest thing she had to friend among her peers, though in many ways she was Coach Fink's opposite. She addressed her equestrians in a quiet, measured voice, ate her cheese sandwiches in tiny, measured bites, crossed the quad in measured, nimble steps. On horseback, Lucille was all elegance and precision, urging her mount toward a rail, hands and knees communicating her desire, then suddenly up and over and gliding together through the landing, coiling together for the next jump. She was, however, a regular at basketball games and field hockey matches, and Coach Fink had never been much good at making friends.

She tracked Lucille down at the stables before basketball practice. Lucille was oiling bridles in the tack room, the walls hung with reins and saddles and photographs of past Briarwood equestrians leaping horses over hedgerows or posed atop their mounts with blue ribbons pinned to their lapels.

"That's an easy one," Lucille said. "The letter represents a message from your subconscious."

"How do you know that?"

"Everybody knows that. You might also consider the possibility that the letter is a pun on 'let her.'"

A symptom of Coach Fink's grogginess: delayed reaction. She was aware of Lucille's words rattling around in her head, but it took them a few seconds to settle for sorting and processing. It was a bit like having someone throw a ball in your direction, recognizing the ball for what it was, anticipating its trajectory, understanding that you were meant to catch it, but finding your hands still hanging at your sides when the ball hit you in the chest.

"I don't know how that helps me," Coach Fink said.

Before Lucille could reply, a student named Grace LaPointe poked her head into the tack room, dirt smudged on her chin. She'd tried out for field hockey last season but failed to make the team. Coach Fink couldn't remember why she'd cut her.

"We're finished," Grace said.

"The horses have been brushed?"

"Yes, ma'am."

"You swept the barn?"

"Yes, ma'am."

"Well, here," Lucille said, offering Grace the bridle in her hands. Several more waited on a hook. "Oil the rest of these, and then you may be excused."

Another thing Coach Fink admired about Lucille, she didn't coddle the girls. If they wanted to be on the riding team, they were required to scrape hooves and muck stalls and so forth, even at a place like Briarwood.

The dreams had started around the same time the Drama Club began rehearsing *The Phantom of Thornton Hall*. This connection was not lost on Coach Fink, but she tried not to think about it as she put the cast through their paces later that evening. She crouched a few feet from the actors, just left of center stage, hands on her knees, a whistle on a string dangling from her neck.

"I remember it snowed for three days straight," Juliet Demarinis was saying in the role of Eleanor Bowman's ghost. She laughed. Too loud, Coach Fink thought. Demarinis compensated for her lack of talent with enthusiasm. "We made a snowman and named him Zacharias after the prophet in the Bible."

"I wish it would snow right now," Thessaly Roebuck replied as Jenny March. Coach Fink had let her have the part because she was the only one who wanted it, but she was already regretting her decision. The girl acted as if she was reciting from an instruction manual. "I'd lie down to sleep and let the snow cover me up and no one would find me until the spring."

Of the three actors in the scene, the only one who struck Coach Fink as reasonably convincing was Littlefield, playing Bridget, and all she had to do was pretend to be asleep. The set was simple—a brass lamp on a nightstand, a pair of old beds they'd found in storage. Eventually they would hang a window frame in the background. All according to directions in the script. Littlefield curled on her side with her knees drawn up, her back to the actors, her lips just slightly parted. Jenny and Eleanor had these weird and rambling late-night conversations, but somehow Bridget was never disturbed. That didn't make a lot of sense to Coach Fink, but what did she know about the rules of stagecraft or the mechanics of conversing with the dead?

She blew a long note on her whistle and shouted, "Cut," her favorite part so far about directing a play. She pointed at a sign hanging in the wings.

To Roebuck, she said, "Read that."

"The sign?"

"Read it," Coach Fink said.

Roebuck fixed her eyes on the sign for a few seconds before returning her attention to Coach Fink. Another symptom of

Coach Fink's grogginess: irritability. Even more sudden and intense than usual. She could feel herself heading toward a boil.

"I mean," she said, "out loud."

"Cast and crew only backstage."

"Do you hear yourself?"

Roebuck blinked and crossed her arms, and Coach Fink could tell that she was on the verge of tears.

"I guess so."

"That right there, that's how you sound saying your lines."

Only the stage was lit, the rest of the auditorium draped in shadow. The girls not currently in the scene gawked from the front row, the lot of them exuding a taut, anticipatory silence. Demarinis pushed up from the bed and put her hand on Roebuck's shoulder.

"It's a metaphor."

"What are you talking about?" Coach Fink said.

"The snow," she said, "it's a metaphor for death. I was just trying to give Thessaly a context for the scene."

If this had been field hockey or basketball practice, Coach Fink would have sent them both off running laps. Through all this Littlefield had stayed in character. Her breathing was shallow, her forehead smooth. She looked so peaceful that, without thinking, Coach Fink reached out and touched her hip. Littlefield rolled onto her back, throwing one arm over her head. Her eyelids fluttered. After a moment, she pushed up on her elbows.

"Did I miss my cue?" she said.

My Lord, Coach Fink thought, she really was asleep. This should have induced a tirade but instead it filled her up with envy. It sounded so pleasant to stretch out on one of those old beds and give in to her grogginess, leave the world behind. She doubted very much that Littlefield was nagged by dream messages from her subconscious. She covered her eyes with her left hand and pictured Roebuck and Demarinis running laps around the auditorium. There would be no more talk of metaphor with those two out there huffing in the cold. This idea calmed her. She could feel her pulse winding down. The muscles in her jaw relaxed.

"Do you know Jenny's lines?" she said.

"I don't think so," Littlefield said. "Not by heart."

Coach Fink squatted down beside the bed.

"If I, as Eleanor's ghost, was to say to you, as Jenny, 'Be wary when you wish for sleep,' what would you say in reply?"

"I'd say, 'I have never been a wary girl.'"

"Two points," Coach Fink said.

In addition to everything else, the loss to Saint Mary's of the Green meant that her basketball Vixens—a mascot that had probably seemed innocent enough in the first half of the century but that the students wore these days with a kind of tawdry, ironic pride—had finished the regular season 12–12, barely making the playoffs. They were slated to tip off against the number-two seed, Port Royal Country Day, and if they didn't tighten up their zone in a hurry, they'd get their butts whipped. So, after rehearsal, Coach Fink jogged Shady Dell Loop—eight laps or 6.4 miles; she'd measured it with the odometer on her pickup—showered, retrieved a bottle of peppermint schnapps from the freezer, and sipped it on the couch while watching a videotape of Port Royal dismantling

Belle Meade Academy. Usually she broke down game film in her office—she had a TV and a VCR set up on a trolley for just that purpose—but it was lonely in the gym at night. She slugged the schnapps. She hoped a few shots might dull her mind enough to keep the dream from coming back. She was on her third pull from the bottle when the doorbell rang. She paused the tape, cinched her robe.

Two surprises met her on the stoop: first, no one was there, and second, it was snowing, big wet flakes sifting out of the night and spinning illuminated past the streetlamps. Like most athletes, Coach Fink was deeply superstitious, inclined to read the weather as a portent. She stepped into the yard and spread her arms and tipped her chin up, snow brushing her wrists, her cheeks. Seen from that angle, the snow appeared to be plummeting straight out of the universe, and she felt oddly but not unpleasantly removed from the laws of time and space. Even as the flakes caught in her lashes she remembered the sensation of snow catching in her lashes, and even as the flakes melted on her tongue she remembered the sensation of snow melting on her tongue. Faintly, as if from memory, she heard students laughing and calling across the quad, discovering the snow. Not much accumulation yet beyond a dusting on the blacktop. Her feet were getting cold.

On her way back inside, she noticed an envelope on the doormat, a third surprise. She'd missed it before, distracted by the snow, and she carried it back to the couch and slipped a thumbnail under the flap and removed a folded sheet of loose-leaf paper scrawled with the words *Your breath stinks of LL's pussy*. Purple ink. There was something else—insect legs of hair nested in one corner of the envelope. Pubic, she assumed. Coach Fink remembered this feeling as well, an interval of stunned emptiness before the hurt seeped in. Not hard to guess the culprit. Thessaly Roebuck had fled the auditorium in tears when Coach Fink replaced her. She doubted Roebuck had the guts all by herself, but surely someone in the Drama Club was responsible. She brought the bottle up, the schnapps sweet on her tongue, harsh in her throat. On TV, paused in time, Port Royal was unleashing a full-court press, and Coach Fink marveled at their spacing.

After a while, she dozed off tipsy on the couch, and the videotape played itself out, fading to static, and the dream returned in altered form. In this version, the letter had arrived. It was waiting in the mailbox, but the gravel lane was so long that Coach Fink walked and walked and never reached the end. And outside, while Coach Fink dreamed, the snow kept drifting down, late in the season for this part of Virginia but not so unusual that anyone was particularly concerned.

VII

After Mr. Bishop's class, when the corridors were jammed and buzzing and everyone was hurrying to lunch, Lenore told Poppy and Melissa that she needed to retrieve a chemistry assignment from her room before fifth period, then slipped across the snowy quad and up the hill to Thornton Hall, nobody the wiser about her lie. The common room was deserted at this hour. No voices. No footsteps. No music drifting under doors.

"Anybody home?" Lenore said.

As if in answer to her question, the phone rang. For privacy, the dorm extension was tucked into a sort of closet off the common room, and Lenore hesitated a moment, a second ring pealing off now, the sound muted because the door to the phone closet was closed. Among the residents of Thornton Hall, it was a point of honor that the phone should never go unanswered, so Lenore turned and hustled over.

"Hello?" she said, but all she heard was static. "Hello?"

The phone was mounted on the wall, an old, decommissioned pay phone that no longer required money to make a call. There was no chair, and the cord was too short to sit on the floor, the idea being that if the girls couldn't get comfortable they'd keep their conversations brief. All around her, the walls were scribbled with phone numbers and doodles and cryptic epigrams. Someone had written *Colin McRose has genital warts*, someone else *Dear God help me please*. Lenore hung up and started for the stairs, but the phone rang again when she reached the landing. She let it ring three times before dashing back to pick it up. "Hello?" she said, but there was just more static on the line, the sound like wind or whispers. She banged the phone onto its cradle and hurried to the second floor.

A marker board on Grace and Bunny's door counted down the days until spring break. Only fifteen left. Most of the girls were headed off to Kiawah or Nags Head or Tybee Island, family homes at the beach, but a few of the girls had more exotic plans—Bermuda, Antibes. Lenore had told her mother she'd been invited to spend spring break in DC with the Chens. Her mother loved Melissa. So polite, so studious. Lenore's father had relocated to Boston with his new wife, Willow, and their twin boys, Matt and Sam. He wasn't interested in her spring break plans. She'd made an appointment at a clinic on E Street. She would check into a hotel, show up for the procedure, spend the rest of the week watching pay-per-view and ordering room service. Her grandmother, her father's mother, had opened a savings account for her the year she was born, and nobody ever bothered to check the balance except Lenore. She would withdraw enough to cover her expenses but not enough to call attention to the transaction, and she would pay for everything in cash, like in the movies. She planned to phone home every couple of days to keep her mother at ease. If she got caught, all she had to do was cook up another lie, maybe something about a Georgetown boy, something punishment-worthy but less complicated than the truth.

She checked the bathroom. Peeked into showers, toilet stalls. Somebody had left her retainer on the ledge above the sink. The fluorescents flickered and hummed. The phone rang again as Lenore stepped into the hall. She held her breath and counted the rings. Six rings, seven. After eleven, the phone went quiet and she exhaled. She stood at the door of her room, shaking her arms loose at her sides, the way she did when she was waiting for the ref to pass her the ball before a free throw.

"Let's get this over with," she said.

She knelt to fish the Ouija board from under Juliet's bed.

"Oh spirits," she moaned, but the campfire solemnity of her voice made her wince. She decided to dispense with the spooky rigmarole. She cleared her throat and began again. "It's me. It's Lenore Littlefield. Sorry to bother you. I'm sure you've got better things to do. Or maybe you don't. Now that I'm thinking about it, being dead is probably pretty boring."

Elizabeth Archer wasn't the only ghost allegedly haunting the school. Briarwood Manor was supposed to be vexed by the one-legged phantom of a Union colonel who'd died on an operating table in the dining room. And Norma Blackford, for whom the freshman and sophomore dorm was named, was rumored to appear to students on occasion, especially when they were engaged in unladylike behavior such as gossip or masturbation. And Pal, a former headmaster's beloved springer spaniel, was reputed to roam the grounds at night, though she didn't suppose you could contact a ghost dog with a Ouija board, assuming you could contact anything with a Ouija board besides your inner dork.

"I've only done this once before, so give me a break if I do something wrong. The last time I did this you—one of you?—somebody spelled the word *baby*. Like you knew I was pregnant. Nobody else knows. I haven't told anyone, not even the father. Especially not the father. And I was super careful with the test strips and everything. No way Juliet knows. It couldn't have been her. Maybe I should ask if there are any spirits in the room?"

The phone started ringing again downstairs. Lenore kept talking. She didn't know what else to do.

"This has been a weird week," she said. "Day before yesterday, Coach Fink booted Thessaly from Jenny March and gave me the part, and now Juliet's not speaking to me anymore. Ordinarily, I wouldn't care. It's not like we had much to say before. And Juliet can be a pretty big chafe. I guess you know that as well as anyone, the way she's bugging you all the time. Elizabeth, are you there? I need to know if what happened the other night was real. I mean, I'm not an idiot. I know the deal. It's like a trick you play on yourself, right. It was really me spelling the word without realizing it or whatever, but it didn't feel like that. I was scared at first, but then I wasn't anymore. I was sort of glad somebody knew. Is that crazy? Am I talking to myself? It would just be nice to know somebody's listening." She drummed her fingers on the planchette. "Hello?" Lenore said. "Is this thing on?" The phone stopped ringing. Lenore closed her eyes and held herself very still for a moment before returning the Ouija board to its box and shoving the box under the bed.

Outside, snow glittered on the bare branches of the oaks and crusted the roofs of buildings like icing on a display of day-old cakes. The ground was pocked with footprints, thousands and thousands of them, charting the progress of all the girls on campus from the dorms to the dining hall and from the dining hall to class and from class back to the dining hall for lunch. Lenore added her footprints to the multitude, the snow just deep enough to crumble into her saddle oxfords and wet her socks. She was halfway to the dining hall when Mr. Bishop's dog came bounding up beside her. The dog shimmied and wagged, a tennis ball in his mouth. She heard Mr. Bishop's voice from up the hill. "Pickett," he was shouting. "Here, boy." Pickett did not heed his call. Instead, he sat on his haunches and dropped the ball at her feet.

Mr. Bishop trotted over, his breath misting in the cold. "Sorry about that."

"No worries," Lenore said. "I like dogs."

She tried to hand him the ball, but he waved her off. "He wants you to throw it."

Pickett was swiping the ground with his tail, eyes fixed on Lenore. So she cocked her arm and let it fly. The ball sailed through the air, and Pickett bolted after it, his black coat a perfect contrast with the snow. He fetched it up and brought it back, clearly pleased with himself.

"I've got a break after fourth period," Mr. Bishop said. "I usually let him run around a little."

Pickett dropped the ball at her feet again.

"Do you believe in ghosts, Mr. Bishop?"

She could feel him staring at her, wondering about her. The thing about Mr. Bishop was, he wanted to teach you something. That wasn't always the case. Some teachers wanted to entertain or impress you, some wanted you to like them, some just wanted you to behave for an hour and move along. But Mr. Bishop believed what he said in class. He was almost too earnest. Even now, he was giving her question more consideration that it deserved.

"I believe a place can be haunted," he said, "if that's what you mean. By the past or history or whatever. And people, too. People can be haunted. But if you mean actual spirits from the other side, then no, I don't guess I do."

Lenore wiggled her toes inside her shoes.

"Why do you ask?" he said.

"Oh, you know the stories about Thornton Hall."

Mr. Bishop smiled. "Does this mean you've had a run-in with Elizabeth Archer?"

"I'm pregnant," Lenore said.

She hadn't meant to tell him. She felt as startled by her revelation as Mr. Bishop looked, and she had the strange sensation that she might suddenly float up off the ground, her heels lifting out of the snow and then her toes, and she imagined gazing down on Mr. Bishop and his dog, a hovering ghost of herself.

"You can't tell anyone," she said. "You have to promise."

"Lenore," he said.

"I'm serious, Mr. Bishop."

She heard him say, "Lenore, wait. Lenore? We're not finished talking about this, Lenore," repeating her name like an incantation, like it had some power over her, but she was already leaving him behind. The dog padded after her for a few steps, but Mr. Bishop called him back, and this time he obeyed.

VIII

Most mornings, Pickett woke Bishop by panting in his face and thumping his tail against the nightstand, letting him know it was time to go outside. The following morning was no different. There passed a few dreamy minutes, as Bishop prepped the coffee maker and buttoned up his coat, when his mind remained empty but for the prospects of the day. He had a test to give in class—World War I through the Great Depression. And he wanted to get his hair cut before the barber closed. And he needed to swing by the liquor store in Manassas. And then he opened the door, and Pickett went tearing out into the snow, bounding and snuffling and high-stepping like a show horse, and Lenore's secret came back to Bishop, his gaze sweeping over campus like he'd never seen this place before.

He went back inside to shower but realized, mid-shampoo, that he'd forgotten to bring Pickett inside with him. He wrapped himself in a towel and hurried out to collect Pickett, then dried and dressed, and he was tying his shoes when it occurred to him that he hadn't rinsed the shampoo out of his hair. He had to start all over again, and he was running late by the time he made his way down to the quad. If not for the test, the morning might have been a disaster, but all he had to do was pace the aisles while his students scribbled in their blue books. He stewed in his discombobulation until fourth period, but Lenore finished her test early and bolted for lunch before Bishop had a chance to get her alone.

So he descended the stairs to the faculty lounge still bogged down in haziness and uncertainty. From the hive of cubbies on the wall he collected his mail—a catalogue from a textbook publisher, a flyer promoting campus movie night, an offer from a credit card company, and a memo from the office of the headmistress—then dumped the lot of it onto a pile of similar material in the trash. The memo from the office of the headmistress settled on top, and on second thought, Bishop picked it out and looked at it again.

To: Faculty, Staff, and Students
From: Office of the Headmistress
Date: March 4, 1994
Subject: Guest Speaker

All members of the Briarwood community are invited to an assembly at 3:30 p.m. on Friday, March 4, in the Beatrix Garvey Memorial Auditorium to hear remarks from Vernon Plank, Assistant Vice President, Disney Company, regarding the planned construction of the Disney's America theme park. Refreshments will be served.

The faculty lounge was tucked down in the basement of Everett Hall, low-ceilinged and musty, ground-level windows leaking a shabby brown light regardless of the weather or the season, a quality of light in no way improved by three inches of snow heaped against the glass. Most of Bishop's colleagues joined the students in the dining hall for lunch, but there was always a squad of brown baggers lurking in the basement. At a conference table littered with Tupperware and wads of cling wrap were Ida Hornbogen (Speech and Debate), Gay Lambert (Studio Art), Helena Griner (Music), and Pamela Sharp (Latin and Greek). Lionel Higgins (Art History) was slumped in a wingback chair reading the *Washington Post*, previously examined sections discarded on the coffee table. Nearest to Mr. Higgins, peppering a hard-boiled egg, was Angela Finch (Freshman English), her white bun pinned into place by what looked like a knitting needle. The vending machines, the copier, the coat rack, the coffee urn. That shabby brown light washed over everything and everyone, imbuing the scene before Bishop's eyes with the permanence of a sepia-tinted photograph.

"Does anybody know what this is all about?" he said.

Angela Finch glanced up from her egg, her face webbed with fine lines like the insides of an antique vase.

"I believe it says we're having a guest speaker, Lucas."

"I can see that," he said, "but it's this afternoon. That's not a lot of notice."

From behind his newspaper, Lionel Higgins said, "I'll wager this has to do with Eugenia Marsh. She's caused quite a stir in the editorial pages. I'll give her credit. That letter was articulate, if a hair melodramatic."

Lionel Higgins was Bishop's next-door neighbor. He was even older than Angela Finch. It was well known that he taught with his back to the class, facing a projector screen on which slides of famous works of art appeared and disappeared with a click of his thumb. Because of his ruined knees, he was always assigned a classroom on the first floor, and once in a while, when the weather was nice, his more daring students would quietly collect their backpacks and bail out through the open windows. Bishop supposed he couldn't blame them, but the idea of old Mr. Higgins turning to face a half-empty room after his lecture made Bishop's joints go weak.

"She was my student, you know," said Angela Finch.

At the conference table, Ida Hornbogen swiveled in her chair, bunching the loose flesh under her chin. "One of many reasons I'd have thought you a more logical choice to direct the play, Angie. Not only is drama in your field but you taught the girl, for heaven's sake. You knew her personally."

Ida Hornbogen hailed from Marlborough, one of those small English towns that exported pride of place. She'd married a Virginia lawyer twenty years ago, had been teaching at Briarwood almost that long, but her accent remained unsullied. She dressed like an Englishwoman from the movies, especially this time of year—tweed skirts, cable-knit sweaters, thick wool tights. When she drank, she always told the same story about the writer Samuel Pepys, how he'd once stopped in Marlborough and enjoyed its hospitality so well he missed all the carriages to Bath.

Angela Finch held up a finger while she chewed, swallowed, wiped her mouth with a paper napkin. "She was quite good even then. She used to give me poems to read."

"Easily distracted, though," said Lionel Higgins. "Don't forget, Angie, I taught her too. You don't get all the credit.

She had a fine eye, but she was prone to unproductive tangents in discussion."

"That was just her creative spirit."

Then Pamela Sharp chimed in, and Gay Lambert had an opinion about the play, and not one of them knew what Bishop knew. Not one of them could he turn to for advice about Lenore. He felt a stab of anger at Lenore for telling him, then an ooze of guilt for feeling angry. He scowled at the memo in his hand. Vernon Plank. The name sounded made up to Bishop—the gruff but lovable neighbor in one of Disney's movies or, in this case, the slick corporate huckster come to sell them happy lies.

"I hear Coach Fink makes the cast stretch before rehearsal," said Ida Hornbogen in her sly, British schoolmarm's voice. "Perhaps they'll perform in matching tracksuits."

Laughter all around. Except from Bishop. He bought a Snickers from the machine and headed for the door. "Goodbye, Lucas," Angela Finch called to his back. A poster requesting submissions for an essay contest in the *Thorn*, the student newspaper, hung along the wall in the stairwell. The deadline, Bishop noticed, had passed the week before.

Though he would have been unwilling to admit it, the news about Vernon Plank provided a welcome distraction for Bishop. He felt unstuck, the gears of his mind turning again in more familiar ways. He had a difficult time believing that Lionel Higgins was right about the reasons for Plank's visit. An angry letter from a washed-up playwright, no matter how articulate or melodramatic, was unlikely to sound alarm bells down in Orlando or out in Pasadena or wherever Disney had its corporate headquarters, but the more he thought about it, the more Bishop began to see why Disney might want to make its case at Briarwood. Beyond anonymous historians like himself and sad idealists like Eugenia Marsh, neither of whom presented much of a threat, the most likely opponents to a theme park in Prince William County were not the locals but the owners of the grand old houses in more affluent neighboring counties, the gentleman squires and foxhunters and plantation dilettantes who'd bought up all the history in the first place. Those people wouldn't want their property values in the tank or third-rate motels popping up all over the place or minivans clogging up the highways en route from God knows where. And did those landowners and weekend steeplechasers enroll their daughters in the nearby public schools? No indeed. They ponied up and shipped them off to places like Briarwood. Though he hadn't heard much rumbling from his colleagues, it seemed to Bishop that Briarwood had a more immediate stake in this debate as well. No question a theme park would impact the region—massively, permanently—but it was hard to predict the long-term consequences of that impact for the school.

The hours until the final bell sludged by, the whisper of pens on blue books punctuated only by sporadic coughs and sniffles. Bishop tried to take advantage of the time by grading tests from previous classes. Eventually he forced himself to fish Lenore's blue book from the stack. She missed a multiple-choice question about the Black Hand and another about the TVA. There were three essay topics to choose from. Lenore had written about the New Deal. "Leading up to the Great Depression, there were many problems in this country. The stock market crash was a primary cause but bank failures and drought also played a part. With the election of 1932, President Roosevelt set out to fix all that . . . ," and so on to the end, leaving her with a grade of 92. He should have been pleased. He read her essay a second time and then a third, not sure what he hoped to find.

A brass plaque in the lobby maintained that Beatrix Garvey Memorial Auditorium could accommodate 216 people at capacity, but it was well under half full this afternoon, too many teachers with too many lessons to prepare, too many students with too many papers to write, too many people with too many better things to do. According to custom, seniors were granted the privilege of the first few rows, then juniors, and so on back to freshmen, faculty and staff filling out the rest. Bishop dropped into an aisle seat in the back row and scanned the crowd. He spotted Lenore with Poppy Tuttle and Melissa Chen, Poppy in the middle, the others' heads tipped toward hers to hear whatever she was saying.

On the stage, two chairs had been arranged to the right of a lectern emblazoned with the Briarwood crest—a wreath of thorny vines encircling a stately oak. Headmistress Mackey occupied one of the chairs, Vernon Plank, Bishop assumed, the other. The man was not at all the corporate shill Bishop had imagined. He looked more like someone's idea of a favorite professor—bearded, bespectacled, corduroyed—and Bishop was struck by the notion that Disney had culled him from some secret back lot in order to put this particular crowd at ease.

The house lights dimmed, and Headmistress Mackey ticked over to the lectern. She was a formidable woman, Augusta Mackey, pushing seventy, perfect posture still intact, all business from toe to neck but with a mane of white hair that suggested a touch of the sorceress about her. A Briarwood girl herself from 1941 to '44, then a teacher of government and economics from '52 to '61 and assistant headmistress from '61 to '69, she was promoted to headmistress in 1970, the first woman ever to occupy the position, her tenure the longest in Briarwood history.

"Most of you are already aware of Disney's plans to build a historical theme park in Prince William County," she began, and Bishop listened for a hint of endorsement or disapproval in her tone. "Our guest today, Mr. Vernon Plank, an assistant vice president for project development, has offered us a glimpse behind the curtain, to use his words. Let us give Mr. Plank our complete attention and our warmest Briarwood welcome."

While the audience clapped and Headmistress Mackey made way at the lectern for Vernon Plank, shaking hands in the exchange, a projector screen descended behind them, the same screen the students used for campus movie night, illuminated now with an artist's rendering of an enormous blue bald eagle, wings widespread, trailing red-and-white-striped bunting from its talons as if carrying it through the sky. Emblazoned in gold letters over the top of this image were the words *Disney's America*.

"Thank you, Dr. Mackey, and thanks to all of you out there." He shaded his eyes to peer at the audience through the bright stage lights. "Thank you for welcoming me today. Yes,

I work for Disney, and yes, Disney is a great big corporation, but we're also more than that. We're an American corporation, our history woven into the fabric of this great nation. We want not only to honor the past but to reach forward into the future, build on that history, make something even better for tomorrow." As he spoke, the images on-screen began to switch every few seconds, from a field of corn to an assembly line, from a family picnic to the steeple of a church backdropped by cloudless sky, and Bishop pictured a team of Disney dwarfs whistling while they worked the controls in the projector room.

"As our nation grows and changes," said Vernon Plank, "we at Disney are constantly reminded, not only of how far we've come but also how far we still must go before we can live up to the promise of democracy. Disney's America offers a promise as well. We promise to celebrate those qualities that have always been a source of our strength and a beacon of hope to people everywhere."

The image on-screen shifted again, another artist's rendering, this time an aerial view of the park, bustling, alive, already populated with thousands of guests. Vernon Plank explained that Disney's America would be divided into territories built around a body of water called Freedom Bay, each territory portraying a different historical period. "The idea," said Vernon Plank, "is not simply to entertain but to educate." With that, he began to highlight some of the major attractions, including a white-water rapids ride, an Underground Railroad experience, an industrial-revolution-themed roller coaster, and daily battle reenactments. "While you sit in the grandstands, you can eat nachos and drink a cold Coke and watch soldiers give their lives for their country just like they did at the real battle of Manassas. Of course, in those days, the audience didn't have nachos or Coke, and dead soldiers didn't rise to take a bow at the end of the show."

Polite laughter from the crowd. Bishop was clutching the arms of his seat. He looked where Lenore was sitting, but he couldn't tell one girl from another in the faint light from the screen.

"The point," Vernon Plank was saying, "is that Disney's core mission has always been greater than entertainment. As a way of showing our support for educational institutions like Briarwood, institutions whose students will lead our country into the future, I am pleased to announce that I have in my pocket a check for fifty thousand dollars, seed money for a new computer lab."

So that's it, Bishop thought. That explained why Headmistress Mackey was willing to play along. What currently passed for Briarwood's computer lab consisted of a dozen word processors set aside for student use in Ransom Library. Since last fall, she'd been gearing up for a fund-raising campaign. Vernon Plank patted the air, tamping down a lazy roll of applause. He said he had time for a few questions, and students began to queue up behind a microphone at the bottom of the left-hand aisle.

Thessaly Roebuck was the first student to reach the mic. She wanted to know if Disney had planned any movie tie-ins with the new park, and Vernon Plank was pleased to announce that, yes, in fact, an animated feature about Pocahontas was already in production.

Next up was Poppy Tuttle. If Bishop had been able to see even a few minutes into the future, he would not have chosen that moment to make an early exit, but he had other things on his mind, and as Poppy stooped her lips close to the mic, he was already slouching toward the doors and out into the snow, sure he'd heard enough.

Question 3

In March of 1994, an organization called Hello Disney, composed primarily of local business leaders and politicians, released a report estimating the positive economic impact of Disney's America on Prince William County. Which of the following was/were among their projections?

A) 12,000 new jobs with an annual payroll of $295 million.

B) 10 million yearly visitors to the park.

C) $1.2 billion in total revenue.

D) All of the above.

IX

The office of the headmistress looked out over the quad, with its stone benches and old oaks, the same benches and oaks Augusta Mackey had rested upon and strolled beneath when she was a student at Briarwood School for Girls, their very presence a reminder that, despite the necessity of progress, some things were built to last. Yes, there would be challenges along the way—such was the nature of life—but challenges could be met and overcome, and if one brought to bear all the savvy and gumption at one's disposal, progress and permanence did not have to be mutually exclusive. Her history with the school was a perfect example. She'd matriculated to Briarwood at the tag end of the summer of 1941, the whole planet burning beyond the gates—the Japs would soon bomb Pearl Harbor, and the Krauts were battering Leningrad—but here, beneath those oaks, the girls went on reading *The Iliad* and *Romeo and Juliet*. That didn't mean they were isolated from history. They had organized bandage-making parties almost every weekend, the fruits of which were shipped to the Red Cross and from there, presumably, overseas, where they might stanch the bleeding of wounded patriots. Or take her first years as headmistress, the Summer of Love barely in the past, not even history yet, Watergate looming in the not-too-distant future, the idea of single-sex education under siege as a relic of a time whose time had passed. Did she batten down the hatches to bar the winds of change? No, she did not. She raised money for scholarships, pushed for diversity in admissions. Ignoring change was no kind of education. Situating the wisdom of tradition within the turbulence of time—that was the way to proceed. And it was exactly the reason she had allowed the Drama Club to proceed with *The Phantom of Thornton Hall*, despite her personal aversion to the material, and courted Disney, despite her distaste for the sort of mindless recreation they were peddling. Permanence meets progress. The play provided a noteworthy connection to Briarwood's past, and a new computer lab kept them squarely on a competitive course into the future. She'd expected a measure of resistance from the board of trustees, always slow to adapt, but not from one of her own students. Standing at the row of windows behind her desk, Headmistress Mackey watched the girls bustling across the quad to breakfast, all of them, whether they realized it or not, citizens of both a new world and the old.

The intercom sounded on her desk. "Mr. Bishop is here!" Her secretary, Valerie Beech, chirped about new arrivals in the anteroom the way other people bleated banalities like "Have a nice day!" Headmistress Mackey was in favor of cheerfulness but not at the expense of dignity. She had, however, learned to live with Valerie's false brightness and exclamation points because there were certain arcane processes and procedures required to run the school that no one but Valerie understood. For instance, it had been Valerie who reminded her that she couldn't suspend Poppy Tuttle without convening a meeting of the Disciplinary Committee, a formality, to be sure, but a nuisance nonetheless.

The door swung open, and Valerie shooed Bishop in with a laugh and swat on the bicep like he'd just said something cheeky, though clearly he had said no such thing. He looked as if he'd been rousted from bed for an interrogation, which, in a way, he had been. Poppy Tuttle would be arriving at nine. Headmistress Mackey had planned to call her parents, give her a thorough dressing-down, and send her packing for the rest of the semester, but since the Disciplinary Committee would have to be involved, she'd decided to gather what facts she could. And it wouldn't hurt to find out exactly what sort of sedition had been fomented in Bishop's classroom. If he'd been putting ideas in Miss Tuttle's head, Headmistress Mackey ought to know about it, despite the fact that no amount of rabble-rousing by a teacher excused her behavior at the assembly. She'd instructed Valerie to have Bishop in her office before first period on Monday morning, and here he was.

"Your tie is crooked," she said, as Bishop lowered himself into one of the spindle-backed chairs on the other side of the desk. And his shirt was wrinkled, and his hair, still damp from the shower, was mussed, and she spotted a smear of dried shaving cream on his earlobe, but she'd learned from experience that people had a saturation point when it came to criticism beyond which they heard nothing at all. You had to pick your battles—a philosophy that applied equally well to the endless give-and-take between permanence and progress. Still standing, she lifted a framed photograph from her desk: her husband, Linwood, at the tiller of his sailboat, the *Augusta*, which he kept moored at a marina down in Portsmouth.

"Do you sail, Mr. Bishop?"

"Well, I've *been* sailing," he said, tugging at his tie, "if that's what you mean, but I can't say that I *sail* per se, no, ma'am."

"You probably know that my husband sails competitively, though age has put his America's Cup dreams to rest." She chuckled fondly and returned the photograph to its place beside the intercom. "If he were here, Mr. Bishop, I'm sure he would tell you that piloting a high-performance sailboat through erratic winds and tricky seas requires a tremendous amount of teamwork. Each member of the crew must be absolutely certain that he can rely on his mates to do their jobs. Do you follow me?"

"Teamwork," he said. "Yes, ma'am."

"I presume you know why you're here this morning?"

He stared at her, a glaze of wary panic in his eyes, as if he suspected that her question was a trap.

"I'm guessing this has to do with Poppy Tuttle?"

"You guess correctly," she said, and she would have sworn he looked relieved. She lowered herself, finally, into the chair behind her desk, taking a last glance at the photograph of her husband. Linwood had been such a source of strength to her over the years. She knew he'd pursued her for her money in the beginning—her great-great-great-grandfather had founded a shipbuilding concern in Norfolk, and though the company had been liquidated before she was born, the proceeds, properly managed, ensured that her family would be taken care of for generations—but they had arrived at a mutual respect akin to, perhaps more potent than, romantic love. Linwood did not begrudge her devotion to her role as headmistress, and she did not begrudge his preference for spending time on his sailboat or riding horses at the Arbor, her family's plantation in Kilmarnock. If anything, separation made their weekend reunions that much more fond. And Linwood was brilliant at fund-raisers and with the board of trustees, his reputation as a sailor verging on genuine renown, his charm balancing her tendency toward abruptness and practicality. Her only regret was that he'd never managed to give her a child, a failing she'd long ago forgiven him.

"More specifically," she said to Bishop, "you are here because Miss Tuttle suggested, during her outburst at the assembly, that you've been discussing Disney's America in class."

Bishop bobbed his head like he'd considered the question in advance. "I thought it would be interesting, you know, keep all those dates and place-names from getting boring, sort of link the history to their lives."

"I've always thought of history as the great drama of civilization writ large. It's only boring, Mr. Bishop, if you allow it to be so. *You know?*" These last words she spoke in italics. She'd always detested that tic of speech. If a person felt compelled to ask, then the odds were that, no, she did not, in fact, *know* or sympathize. *Sort of* was equally inane. A thing either was or it was not, and qualifying modifiers didn't change the facts. "Isn't that your job, to make history relevant and exciting for the girls?"

"That's what I was trying to do."

"Am I to understand, then, that you find history itself so inadequate to your needs that you feel compelled to inject personal opinion into your lectures, regardless of the consequences?"

"I only meant that—"

"I know what you meant. What I fail to comprehend is how slavery and the forced relocation of indigenous peoples, both subjects referenced by Miss Tuttle, can't be made interesting for our girls without allusion to the Disney Company."

Bishop pressed his lips together and shifted his gaze to a point just to the right of her head. There was something he wanted to say—she could see that. The windows in her office faced due east, and as a result it was possible to judge the hour of the morning, allowing for seasonal variations, by the way in which the sun cast her shadow on the wall opposite her desk. At this particular time of year, the sun seeped over the horizon around seven o'clock, casting no shadow at all, was high enough to shine drowsily into her office by eight, her shadow a dim ghost of its future self, but by nine, the light was burning into her window, her shadow long and dark and imposing, her physical self, she imagined, rimmed with luminosity like the moon during a solar eclipse, radiance catching in her hair, that light beaming simultaneously into the eyes of whoever had the misfortune to be sitting on the other side of her desk. At this moment, behind Bishop, the shadows were just beginning to coalesce, not yet recognizable as herself or Bishop or anything else, reluctant gradations of light and dark, which put the hour somewhere shy of eight o'clock.

"Speak your mind," she said.

"I'm sorry. I left the assembly early. I heard everything secondhand. Did Poppy really call him a—" He stopped short of the word itself.

"*Douche*, Mr. Bishop. Try not to seem so amused."

"But you can't actually think this theme park is a good idea?"

"What I think or do not think is irrelevant, just as your attitude toward potential donors is irrelevant to the way in which history is discussed in your classroom. The question, in this instance, is not historical in the least. At issue is the future of this school."

"But that's—" he began, and then he reined himself in a second time. He was right to reconsider. She was in no mood to debate, especially about an issue that had weighed on her mind so heavily and for so long.

"Let me save us both a little time and possibly save you a great deal of regret. You might be inclined to argue that the presence of this theme park puts the future of the school in jeopardy, but if you think that I have not considered every possible ramification then you quite underestimate me, Mr. Bishop. Perhaps you have forgotten that I have been affiliated with Briarwood in one way or another for half a century. My own history and the history of this place are one and the same. I am confident that our foundation is built on bedrock, more than sturdy enough to bear whatever change the years might bring. This institution has weathered far greater storms than Disney. Better to ally ourselves with the agent of change than to have no control at all. You might also be preparing to make the case for historical accuracy, but you know as well as

I do that history is just a story we tell ourselves about the past and has only the loosest relationship to the truth. Disney's version of that story is insignificant in the long run. Do I wish this theme park were not going to be built? Of course. Do I foresee a way in which Briarwood can successfully prevent it? I do not." She steepled the tips of her fingers beneath her chin. "Have I done justice to your arguments?"

"You've got the gist," he said.

"We have to consider the big picture, Mr. Bishop. I should think that a historian would be aware of that. Besides, for all we know, Disney's America will turn out to be the very best thing, exactly the right thing, for Prince William County and for this school."

Bishop cupped his hands over his knees and looked at the floor between his feet. "What will happen to Poppy?"

"It is my intention to see that Miss Tuttle is suspended following the requisite meeting of the Disciplinary Committee."

"Doesn't that seem a little harsh?"

"This is not her first offense, Mr. Bishop, and even if that were not the case, insulting a guest of this school at a public assembly, the representative of a donor no less, by referring to him as a feminine hygiene product would be unacceptable behavior to say the least, deserving of stern and immediate punishment." Even as she spoke, her eyes still boring down on Bishop, she was aware of Linwood, tan and beaming on her periphery like one of those movie stars the past few generations seemed incapable of producing, a leading man whose magnetism was only enhanced by time.

"Look," Bishop said, "I raised the subject of Disney's America in class. Maybe I shouldn't have—I don't know—but there's no way Poppy would have done what she did at the assembly if I hadn't."

"There's plenty of blame to go around." Headmistress Mackey stood, leaning forward slightly in order to loom with greater presence. "I believe you have a class to teach. You're on to World War II if I'm not mistaken. If you insist on incorporating real-world lessons into your discussion, I'm sure the subject of teamwork would prove invaluable to the girls, perhaps something about Churchill and Roosevelt."

As if on cue, the bell began to chime, tolling Bishop out the door.

Headmistress Mackey passed the hour between Bishop's departure and Miss Tuttle's arrival composing a letter to potential donors, those alumnae most likely to see a new computer lab for what it was—not as an indulgence but as a necessity—her shadow gradually solidifying on the wall, the impression of her hair like some wild jungle plant opening in the sun. She'd written hundreds of similar letters in her career, and so, as she composed, she was able to simultaneously disappear into the back room of her thoughts where she considered the rogues' gallery of students she had been forced to suspend or expel over the years, the majority for cheating, though there had been a handful of students she'd sent home for drinking or smoking pot or, more often, as in Miss Tuttle's case, some conglomeration of disciplinary concerns, perhaps two dozen girls in all, half again that number if you included her time as assistant headmistress, a short list, really, given the length of her tenure, each case difficult and disappointing, none more so than Eugenia Marsh, suspended for smuggling a Woodmont boy into her room after an on-campus production of *The Seagull* by Anton Chekhov.

Even among the older faculty, time had blotted out that detail of Eugenia Marsh's record, a collective lapse of memory further blurred by the glitter of her Pulitzer Prize, but Headmistress Mackey had not forgotten. Eugenia Marsh had been such a bright young woman and so talented but also erratic and impulsive, incapable of distinguishing authentic self-expression from pure mulishness. How could Headmistress Mackey forget—how could any of them?—the day Eugenia Marsh had worn her bra outside her blouse to class, arguing later that she was still within the confines of the dress code. What had she accomplished? Not one thing, except to compel an absurdly specific revision of the dress code. And there was the incident with the bell tower and that business in the trophy room. Headmistress Mackey shuddered to recall. It was not infrequently the case that suspended students decided not to return, seeking instead a fresh start at a school better suited to their personalities, but Eugenia Marsh had returned for her senior year. To Headmistress Mackey's surprise, she came back changed, humbled, proof that punishment might lead to rehabilitation. She caused not a lick of trouble for the school until that mixed blessing of a play.

Headmistress Mackey scrawled a closing on her letter and dropped the letter in her outbox for Valerie to collect and type this afternoon. She checked her shadow on the wall—denser, more distinct, a near-perfect silhouette. She was about to buzz Valerie on the intercom when she heard a voice rising from below. She couldn't decipher the words, but the sound was cadenced and robust, repeating like a chant. She pushed to her feet and faced the windows, the light so bright she had to shade her eyes to make out Poppy Tuttle, sign propped on her shoulder, marching on the quad.

X

Down with Disney, the sign had read, a slogan so obvious it failed to impress Lenore. The Disciplinary Committee was scheduled to meet on Friday, an expedited hearing, and when Lenore let herself imagine how the hearing might play out, a lump of fearful anger bellied up in her throat.

Tonight she was following Poppy and Melissa on their rounds of the library. They were still working off their service hours. Melissa pushed a book-laden cart with a bum wheel from row to row, the wheel stuttering a rubbery sticking noise every few rotations, like the cart had something to say but couldn't spit it out. Poppy, on the other hand, had no such hesitation.

"There are only two kinds of women in those movies—insipid beauties and crazy witches. That's it. Either you're sweet and submissive and enjoy cleaning house and singing to birds and rodents and dwarfs, in which case you require a man to come to your rescue when the shit hits the fan, or you're pathological with vanity and jealousy and bent on the destruction of your prettier counterparts." Every now and then, while she spoke, Poppy would select a book from the cart and, without checking the title or author or call number, press it into a gap on one of the shelves. "Aurora and Maleficent, Snow White and the evil queen, Cinderella and her step-bitches, Ariel and the big fat squid woman."

"Ursula," Lenore said.

"Right, Ursula. The point is we're being brainwashed young. Helpless or horrible, those are our choices according to Disney. Two of those princesses are so pathetic they snooze through their own movies waiting for a handsome prince to kiss them back to life."

From somewhere behind the stacks a peal of laughter fluttered up and away beneath the vaulted ceiling. Ransom Library resembled nothing so much as a cathedral—weathered stone, arched windows, Gothic details; the only thing missing was a steeple—but Lenore had once heard Mr. Higgins remark that its closest architectural model was a prison, on the inside at any rate: three stories, each floor a gangway lined with shelves and overlooking the study area and the circulation desk on the ground level. Overhead, a pair of enormous chandeliers scattered shards of light. That laughter bubbled up again, the sound so bright and insubstantial it might have been coming from the chandeliers, but no one seemed to notice except Lenore.

"Ariel's not so bad," Melissa said.

"Give me a break. Ariel literally gives up her voice for the love of a man she's laid eyes on for like fifteen seconds total. Her voice—hello?"

Lenore had been amazed, even proud, when Poppy stood up in front of the whole auditorium to challenge Vernon

Plank. She couldn't recall every detail of their exchange, but she remembered the way his hand had gone to his heart like Poppy had hurt his feelings. "I can assure you that we aren't ignoring anything, young lady. In fact—and I'm giving you a genuine sneak preview here—by employing the very latest in virtual-reality technology, Disney Imagineers have created an Underground Railroad experience so revolutionary that it will really make you feel what it was like to be a slave." That's when Poppy called him a douche. And you couldn't blame her. Setting aside the lameness of the term *Imagineers*, what kind of person believed that you could re-create the experience of slavery in a theme park ride? What Lenore couldn't get her head around was why Poppy cared. Or why she was pretending to care. This whole line of discussion felt a little rehearsed to Lenore, a little overstated.

"You forgot Belle," she said. "She's not a princess. She's smart. She saves her dad."

"Belle—shit. She might be the worst of all. Disney wants us to believe that Belle's all independent and strong, but she willingly becomes the prisoner of a monster. And then she falls in love with him. Really? Sounds like Stockholm syndrome to me, but the movie still ends with a wedding."

Lenore lifted a book from Melissa's cart. The cover was stained and battered, the title worn away. According to the checkout sheet, the book had been most recently in the possession of Astrid Lewis, a senior. Lenore didn't know her except by sight—pale blonde, willowy, pretty from a distance, but up close you noticed that her eyes were crossed. Before Astrid, the book had last been checked out eight years ago by someone called Regan Pierce and before that by Gretchen Beattie and Flora Stein and Agnes Key, all the way back to Stella Brighthouse, Lenore's grandmother. For almost half a century her signature had lived in this book in its place upon these shelves, to be discovered or not by some girl or other, the book read and returned and checked out again and so on, until this moment, Lenore selecting just this book from Melissa's cart while Poppy rambled about her gripe with Disney, a perfectly ordinary sequence of events, capped by a coincidence that struck Lenore as profound.

"I'll be right back," she said.

Lenore left her friends in World Literature and hurried down to the basement where the stacks were metal instead of wood, the lighting all wan fluorescence. On a row of shelves facing the back wall of the building, she located past editions of *The Green and White*. It had occurred to Lenore that she might hunt up a photograph of Elizabeth Archer in the yearbook, an idea that made her heart race, as if a yearbook photograph, proof of Elizabeth Archer's presence on campus, proof of her passage though real life, might lend credence to the stories about her ghost. She crabbed along the aisle, fighting a sneeze against the dust. But the volumes only dated back to 1925. According to legend, Elizabeth Archer had been a student during WWI. Did they even have yearbooks in those days? Or maybe the earliest editions were too delicate to be handled? And if that was the case, where were they stored? Surely a school as tradition-proud as Briarwood saved old yearbooks for posterity.

Perhaps because they had moved on to WWII in Mr. Bishop's class, Lenore plucked the 1944 edition from the shelf. The dedication read, "To the Heroes of Prince William Military Academy," nineteen of whom, according to the copy, had lost their lives in combat that year alone. Prince William Military Academy had closed its doors long before Lenore's time, but she'd heard her grandmother and her mother reminiscing about formals way back when, handsome boys decked out in military dress. She thumbed deeper into the yearbook. Each girl in the senior class, only twenty-six of them, had a whole page to herself. Poised and smiling, they looked, like all young women in antique photographs, more grown-up than their true ages. Mary Ellen King. Judith Lawrence. Rosemary Magnuson. Augusta Price. Recognition startled Lenore like the photograph had blinked. Headmistress Mackey. Her maiden name. She hadn't been exactly pretty, but she was sure of herself, you could tell, her eyes staring into the camera, her smile suggesting somehow that she knew things you didn't.

Lenore slipped the 1944 edition back into its slot and ran her finger down the row of spines to 1962, Eugenia Marsh's final year at Briarwood. The hairstyles and the poses had changed—instead of head shots and a solid backdrop, the girls were seated on a wrought-iron bench in front of a phony nature scene—but the uniforms were the same. Even then Eugenia Marsh sported what would become her trademark bob. Her hands were folded in her lap, her knees cocked demurely to one side. Nothing about that image hinted at what history had in store. Lenore flipped to Activities and found her again, this time with the Drama Club, hidden in the back row, her face barely visible between two taller girls.

After Eugenia Marsh, Lenore went searching for Coach Fink, skimming years of bad haircuts until she tracked her down in 1976. By then, enrollment was high enough that there wasn't enough room to give every senior her own page, and she found her coach lined up with three other students, second row from the top, last face from the left, her smile so big Lenore almost didn't recognize her, wouldn't have recognized her if not for the freckles. Those braces! Those bangs! That face looked more familiar in the action shots back in Athletics—eyes fierce, lips pressed into a hard, determined line. Before returning the yearbook to the shelf, just out of curiosity, Lenore flipped to the Drama Club, and there was Coach Fink in a white nightgown, holding some boy's hand, her mouth a perfect oval, like an angel's mouth on a Christmas tree ornament. Coach Fink as Maria in *West Side Story*. That helped explain why her basketball coach had been put in charge of *The Phantom of Thornton Hall*, a much-debated mystery among this year's cast, but it was so weird to imagine. Coach Fink onstage, emoting. Lenore clapped the yearbook shut like she had bungled onto something lewd.

She looked up her grandmother—1947—and her mother—1968. Lenore had her grandmother's upturned nose, her mother's brow and chin. All three of them had the same no-nonsense eyes. Seeing her eyes in those old photographs gave Lenore such a case of the creeps that when someone spoke behind her, she gasped and clapped a hand over her stomach and spilled her mother's yearbook from her lap.

"Are you mad at me?" Poppy said.

She was leaning against the wall at the end of the aisle, bathed in the pallid light of the fluorescent bulbs, and at that moment, just as Lenore was settling back into herself, recognizing her friend in the basement instead of some lurking phantom, the lights buzzed and flickered, and one of the long bulbs in the rack over Poppy's head expired.

"Maybe a little."

Poppy shouldered away from the wall, retrieved the fallen yearbook, and handed it to Lenore.

"I don't understand what you're doing," Lenore said. "You're gonna get kicked out of school."

"I don't know what I'm doing either," Poppy said.

"There's too much happening right now," Lenore said. "We've got the Port Royal game tomorrow night. And the play—I've never been in a play before. And now this, you." She bit her bottom lip, forcing herself to hush before her secret came tumbling out again.

"Do you think people can be happy?" Poppy said. "In a general sense, I mean. Like do you think happiness is even possible?"

"What kind of question is that?"

"I don't know." Poppy sat on the floor and wrapped her arms around her knees. "I think we spend so much time pretending that we've forgotten what real happiness feels like anymore."

Lenore heard footsteps. Melissa appeared at the end of the aisle.

"What are we doing down here?"

"Smoking," Poppy said.

She fished around in her peacoat and came out with a pack of Marlboro Lights. Lenore watched her stab a cigarette between her lips and, in no hurry, light up and breathe the smoke into her lungs.

"Fuck it," Poppy said, followed by a long exhale.

Lenore looked at Melissa. Melissa shrugged. There was no point scolding her. Obviously, you couldn't smoke in the library, but nothing Poppy did was likely to make her situation worse. It had not escaped Lenore that she could move in with Melissa when Poppy was gone, be done with Juliet Demarinis, problem solved. So she said nothing, and they sat among the yearbooks and let Poppy puff away, whorls of smoke hanging low over their heads.

XI

The bus trip back from Port Royal was long and quiet, and it was after midnight by the time Coach Fink got the girls off to their dorms. She sat on a bench in the empty locker room trying to absorb the fact of a losing season. Not her first but rare enough and always hard to swallow. 54–21. The score that close only because Port Royal took pity on them down the stretch. She had reached that particular state of exhaustion in which her body was spent but her mind kept racing, as if it had already sprinted past consciousness and entered the revved-up state of a waking dream, a sensation that recalled the actual dream most likely awaiting her in sleep. The only thing she could think to do was jog herself down into another, deeper state of weariness in which her brain shut itself off completely.

A full moon blurred out the stars. Her footsteps on the pavement made a muted thumping sound that seemed independent of her running, as if she were pursued by the ghost of her younger self, woods on her right all the way around to insulate the school from the rest of the world, campus on her left, old buildings slabs of shadow in the moonlight. Coach Fink hated losing. There was no getting around the fact that it happened once in a while, but she believed that if you pushed yourself hard enough, if you did the little things right every day, every hour, every minute, if your focus was clear, if you dedicated yourself to winning, then that's exactly what you would do more often than not. Losing was a habit. Losing was a state of mind. And she had somehow failed to notice it taking hold of her team. Port Royal hadn't just beaten them tonight. They'd broken them, obliterated them. No matter how Coach Fink tweaked the lineup or the game plan—zone defense or man-to-man, half-court offense or full-court press—her players had never believed that they could win, and that lack of belief was Coach Fink's fault.

She'd let herself get distracted by *The Phantom of Thornton Hall*, the envelope on her doorstep. She could see that now, and there was nothing she could do to make it right. The play was better with Littlefield as Jenny, or it could have been, but morale was shot, and Demarinis yawped her lines, and the rest of the cast were even more wooden and lethargic than before. Coach Fink was in over her head. She was aware that this was exactly the sort of defeatist attitude she'd recognized in her players, but she didn't know how to shut it off. She reminded herself that they still had a month of rehearsals. She'd just have to ride them harder. She spurred herself past the student parking lot and the physical plant, steam pluming into the night, but she felt drained empty, as if her will had sprung a leak. She couldn't be sure if this was her fifth or sixth lap around Shady Dell Loop. Even before she knew she was going to stop, she began to slow, hands on her hips, taking in as much air as the night would give. She paced a hundred steps, then turned and paced a hundred more, warming down her legs, and when she counted the last few steps—ninety-eight, ninety-nine—she found herself face-to-face with Lucas Bishop, who was out there with his dog.

"Well," he said, "how'd we do?"

He was wearing a worn waxed field coat over a T-shirt, the beginnings of a belly pressing against the cotton. It took Coach Fink a second to realize that he was asking about the game.

"We got our butts kicked."

"I'm sorry about that." Bishop patted his thigh, and the dog parked itself at his side. "How far did you run?"

"Maybe five miles."

"You're barely even breathing hard."

"I take care of myself," she said, and then she blushed. He was just being nice, she thought, just trying to sidetrack them from the subject of the game. She couldn't be sure if the blush was born of his effort or her pride or the fact that his kindness was just another sort of pity. To cover the blush, she started pacing again, like she hadn't finished warming down. The dog fell into step beside her, and Bishop followed suit.

"What's his name again?" she said.

"Pickett."

"Pickett," she repeated, and the dog gazed up at her as if eager to hear the rest of what she had to say. "I remember this one game my sophomore year. I went 0 for eleven in the first half against Belle Meade. It was like I'd forgotten how to shoot a basketball. It was awful. A nightmare. One thing I was good at in the world and it was gone. The more I missed the worse it got. I thought I'd never sink another basket."

"Let me guess," Bishop said, "you played better in the second half?"

"I bricked my first five shots before Coach Udall benched my ass."

He laughed, and she could feel him looking at her.

"You probably shouldn't use that story in a halftime speech."

"Oh, screw you, Bishop," Coach Fink said. "I shot better in the next one. Dropped a double double on Massanutten."

She kept waiting for him to turn back, but he matched her stride down the hill, Pickett trotting circles around them, tags jangling in the dark.

"How's the play going?" Bishop said.

Coach Fink stopped and glared. "Are you trying to rack my balls?"

Bishop pinched his fingers and drew them across his lips like he was pulling a zipper closed. "I'll just keep it shut," he said.

"I don't even like the play," Coach Fink said, walking again. "It's just girls sitting around a dorm room. They talk and talk and talk, but nothing ever happens. I prefer a little action with my entertainment."

"Isn't one of those girls a ghost?"

"Not a very scary one," Coach Fink said.

Pickett huffed at the scent of horses in the stables as they rounded the bottom of the loop. In the gatehouse, bathed in yellow light, the security guard smoked a cigarette on his stool, his white truck parked in the exit lane. It occurred to Coach Fink that someone observing their progress might have mistaken them for friends.

"The cast hates me," she said.

"I doubt it's as bad as all that."

"They gave me pubes."

"They what?"

"Pubic hair," she said. "In an envelope. They think I'm a lesbian."

Bishop opened his mouth but closed it without speaking.

"You probably thought so, too." Coach Fink socked him on the bicep. "Goddamnit, Bishop. We've been acquainted a long time, but I don't know a thing about you. I don't even know where you're from."

"Richmond," Bishop said, rubbing his arm.

"You play sports?"

"I played baseball in high school."

"What position?"

"First base."

"You any good?"

"I was OK in the field, but I couldn't hit a curve."

"And what are you doing out here?" she said.

"How do you mean? I'm walking my dog."

"It's the middle of the damn night."

Bishop kept his eyes on his feet. Streetlamps spaced Shady Dell Loop every twenty yards or so, causing their shadows to bloom into being, then fade and bloom again, as if they couldn't make up their minds.

"I haven't been sleeping very well."

"Now I know something," Coach Fink said.

They started back up the hill in silence. This side of Shady Dell Loop was higher than the other, built up on a sort of grassy berm, so they were almost level with the darkened second-story windows in the buildings on the quad. From this angle, at this hour, with the moonlight casting everything silver, the buildings appeared miniaturized, like the school was an elaborate scale model of itself.

Pickett pricked his ears at something only he could hear, then ranged off into the woods. Bishop let him go.

"You know what you should do," he said. "You should try to contact Eugenia Marsh."

"And why would I do that? I'd like to strangle that kook."

"I was thinking you could invite her for opening night," Bishop said. "That'd give the girls something to get excited about."

"I thought she was a hermit."

"Things change. She wrote that letter to the *Post*."

For a few long seconds she let herself entertain his proposal—she could practically feel the machinery whirring behind her eyes, could see the looks on the faces of Demarinis and Roebuck and the rest of them—but then her mind blanked, like the idea had tripped a breaker.

"It doesn't matter," Coach Fink said. "I have no idea how to find Eugenia Marsh, and even if I did, she wouldn't come."

She walked backward to work her quads. A few steps behind, with his hands in his coat pockets, Bishop was puffing up the grade, old oaks lining Faculty Row like the canopy of an enormous, ruined tent, moonlight sifting between the branches. Pickett coalesced out of the night and led them all the way back to Bishop's yard.

"You know I played the lead my senior year," Coach Fink said. "Maria. We did *West Side Story*."

She recognized the skepticism in Bishop's silence. "What?"

"Nothing," Bishop said.

Coach Fink drew her braid over her shoulder and gripped it with both hands. She made a noise in her throat, a sort of harrumph, like a scandalized old biddy. Then she began to sing. "There's a place for us . . . somewhere a place for us." She started softly, but as she felt her way into the lyrics, she shut her eyes and let the song unfurl. Hers was not a great voice—she knew that—but it was clear and full, and even she could hear how lovely it sounded on this night. "There's a time for us . . . someday a time for us." The words lifted out of her. She felt them hanging in the air like mist. This had always been her favorite song in the show. She liked how sweet and simple it was, how hopeful, how tragic. "Somehow . . . someday . . . somewhere." Coach Fink held the last note, and then she opened her eyes, and for a moment it was like waking from an impossibly vivid dream, the real world all around her hazy and false.

Bishop was standing close enough to surprise her. Pickett swiped the air with his tail. Headlights cut the darkness along Faculty Row, the security guard making his rounds, the light catching on Bishop's T-shirt. As the truck passed and the darkness settled over them again, Coach Fink shot a hand out and pinched the flab at Bishop's middle, and he made a sound like "Yeef" and clapped his palms over his stomach. She didn't know why she'd done it but she had, and now it was too late to take it back.

"We need to get you out here exercising more often," she said. "Your dog looks pretty good, but you could use a little work."

Then she pivoted and walked away, her cheeks blazing again. But for the sound of her footsteps Shady Dell Loop was quiet. She didn't look back, not once, just kept striding down the row to her place and then up the steps and through the door and into bed, where there waited a dream of mysterious letters and gravel lanes.

XII

Bishop's lesson plan on the day of Poppy's hearing was to divide his students into groups and have them discuss the ethics of the atom bomb, one group in favor, one against, but he had trouble focusing on the debate. He'd been instructed to make himself available to the Disciplinary Committee during his free period in case his testimony was required. While his students spoke, he nodded and made interested noises in his throat, aware that Juliet Demarinis was saying something about the casualties that would have resulted from an invasion of Japan, and Marisol Brooks was saying something about the murder of women and children, and Lenore Littlefield was saying nothing at all. Every time he glanced in her direction, he found her staring out the window, her gaze, he supposed, focused on the Herndon Annex across the quad, where the hearing was already in progress.

He needed to talk to her. Something. Already he'd let a week go by. But the bell chimed the end of class, and the atom bomb was forgotten, the room a hubbub of girlish voices, and he watched Lenore shoulder her backpack and follow Melissa out the door, his blood skittering with a feeling very much like relief. He waited until the building was quiet before shutting off the lights. He figured he had just enough time to let Pickett out for a minute or two before he made his appearance at the hearing.

The snow had melted away, leaving the grounds spongy and damp, so Bishop trailed around Shady Dell Loop instead of cutting up the hill. Faint music drifted over from the student parking lot. A car passed, headed in the opposite direction. The driver honked a greeting, and Bishop waved without looking up from his shoes.

He was refilling Pickett's water bowl when he noticed the message light blinking on his answering machine. He checked his watch, pressed play. For a few seconds, there was only vague rustling, like someone crumpling paper, and then dogs barking—Pickett pricked his ears—and then his father's voice lifted into the room. "Hush, now. It's just the mailman." The voice was firm but distant, as if his father wasn't speaking into the phone, and the dogs went quiet, his father's dogs, Mercy and Rhett. Bishop heard footsteps moving away—his father must have forgotten the phone—and a door opening and closing and behind that a kind of living silence as the tape spooled out. Bishop stared at the machine, wondering what his father was doing home in the middle of the day. He was still with the Department of Corrections, an administrative position now, no longer handling cases.

Beside the phone and the answering machine was a ceramic bowl in which Bishop dropped his car keys and his loose change and whatever else might happen to be cluttering up his pockets, and he noticed, just then, the button Poppy had given him on the battlefield. *FTM*. He picked it up and turned it over in his hand, shaking loose a penny wedged behind the pin. *In case your testimony is required*. That phrase troubled him, particularly the word *required*. He didn't know if his testimony would damn Poppy or exonerate her. In accordance with the bylaws, the committee would be composed of four members: the assistant headmistress (Olivia Proulx, Briarwood class of '71); a representative from the board of trustees (Paul Ransom, whose great-grandmother, Agnes, class of '29, had provided the endowment for the library); a representative from the faculty (Barbara Kline, biology); and an elected representative from the student body (Husna Hesbani, class of '94). Headmistress Mackey would be presiding, but she could only vote to break a tie. All of this was taking place in the Bowles Room, with its wainscoting and its conference tables, its walls lined with portraits of headmasters past. By the time Bishop arrived, Poppy and her parents were waiting on a bench out in the hall. Poppy did introductions, and Bishop shook her father's hand.

"They're deliberating," Poppy told him.

So Bishop's testimony would not be required after all. He dropped onto a matching bench across from the Tuttles.

"That little Indian girl should have recused herself," Poppy's father said.

"Husna's got it in for me," Poppy explained. "She's my RA."

There was something amused in her demeanor, as if the hearing, like so many adult dramas—local elections, foreign wars—had no real bearing on her life, but she was charmed by their concern.

Her father leaned his forearms on his thighs.

"If it doesn't go our way, we'll have grounds for appeal."

"We're not going to appeal," her mother said.

The Tuttles were both blond and blue-eyed, like their daughter, Mr. Tuttle in his gray suit and striped tie, his wing-tips, Mrs. Tuttle in black slacks and a matching tailored coat with brass buttons up the front, black heels. She looked so exactly the way Poppy would look one day that Bishop had trouble meeting her eyes.

Poppy's father said, "They're not going to run my daughter out of here because of some little Indian girl."

"I think Husna's family is from Pakistan," Poppy said, and she gave Bishop a look, like the two of them were in cahoots.

"You just be quiet," her mother said. "Both of you."

Bishop had tucked the button in his breast pocket, and he fished it out and cupped it between his palms. He had thought he might return it to her, but that didn't feel right, so he pinned the button to his lapel, and Poppy beamed at him for a moment. Then the door to the Bowles Room opened, and Valerie Beech peeked out. "We're ready for you now," she said, and it was clear from her expression that deliberations had not gone well.

He had two more classes to teach. He stuck to his lesson plan, listening to his students going back and forth about how many lives were saved and how many more were lost, and afterward he couldn't remember a single word that anyone had said. Poppy had been suspended until the end of the semester. Bishop nicked his mail from the faculty lounge, started for home, then changed his mind halfway up the hill and veered toward Thornton Hall. Grace LaPointe let him in, shouting, "Man in the house." She told him where to find Poppy's room, and Bishop kept his eyes straight ahead as he moved in that direction. He tried not to see anything he shouldn't see. Poppy's father was perched on the bare mattress of her bed, taping a cardboard box. A hunter-green luggage set waited by the door.

"They gave us 'til Monday," he said, "but what's the point?"

Bishop volunteered to help carry Poppy's things out to the car, a Land Rover with Georgia plates parked in the loading area behind the dorm. The two men went about their business without saying much, though every now and then, hefting another box, Poppy's father would marvel at how it was possible to fit so much junk into such a small room. Poppy's mother waited in the Land Rover, the hatch open while they worked, a tiny electric bell pinging and pinging and pinging all the while. Poppy and Melissa and Lenore sat on the curb, talking quietly. Poppy seemed reduced, the moment catching up to her. The image called to mind those roadside sufferers you often passed after an accident. Every time he emerged with a suitcase, Bishop had to resist the temptation to tell someone that if they would take the keys out of the ignition the pinging would cease. When the Land Rover was loaded, the hatch shut, the pinging silenced, Poppy gave her friends a tearful hug and said good-bye to Bishop and climbed into the back seat. Then she jumped out again and threw her arms around Bishop's neck and kissed him on the mouth, startling him, clutching him tight enough to lift her feet off the ground. For an instant, less than that, he felt not desire but the thrill of being desired, and in the very next instant he wrenched his face away and pried her arms free and held her slim wrists in his hands. She stood there, grinning, that amused look on her face, and Bishop understood that she was just messing with her parents. Her mother rolled the window down and said, "Oh for God's sake, Poppy, get in the car," and for once Poppy Tuttle did as she was told.

Bishop found his scale under a pile of dirty towels in the bathroom closet. He couldn't remember the last time he'd weighed himself. The surface was scummed with dark patches roughly the size and shape of his feet. 191 pounds. A little heavier than he would have guessed but not too bad. Pickett studied him through the open door, head on his paws. Bishop stripped to his boxers and tried again. Minus his clothes, he was down to 189, half a dozen pounds more than he'd weighed in college. He gathered the flab between his fingers where Coach Fink had pinched him. Such a strange woman, Coach Fink. With the ball of his foot, Bishop shoved the scale under the sink where it would be easier to locate in the future. He stepped out of the bathroom and shut the door to allow himself access to the full-length mirror bolted to the back. His weight was all right, but he'd sagged and softened in the last few years. *Doughy* was the word that came to mind. His winter pallor didn't help. Somehow the mass from his chest had pooled around his middle. He rolled loose flesh between the thumbs and index fingers of both hands. Pickett's eyes sought Bishop's in their reflection.

"What do you think, buddy?" Bishop said.

The dog followed him into the kitchen, where he plunked ice cubes into a glass and soaked the ice in bourbon, then started a pot of canned chicken noodle on the stove. A toilet flushed next door. In most ways, Lionel Higgins was the perfect neighbor. Besides the plumbing, the only noises Bishop ever heard from over there were muted footsteps or coughing or the murmur of TV or NPR, the exact same sounds he was making on his side. He filled Pickett's bowl with kibble. He let the whiskey burn down his throat and listened to his father's message again. How long had it been since they last spoke? Two weeks? Three? His mother called once a week or so, but she didn't always put his father on. While he waited for the soup to heat, Bishop knocked off eleven push-ups on the floor.

He was reaching a bowl down from the cabinet when the doorbell rang. Pickett stopped eating to listen. For a second, Bishop stood there in the kitchen in his boxer shorts like he didn't recognize the sound.

"Who's there?"

"It's Lenore. Lenore Littlefield."

"Hang on," Bishop said, and he hustled back to the bedroom and dressed himself again, cursing under his breath. He emerged barefoot, his shirttails hanging out. Lenore was sitting on the stoop. Bishop pulled the door shut behind him, Pickett whining on the other side.

"I'm sorry to bother you at home."

"It's all right," he said, sitting beside her. "Today was a bad day."

"I didn't come up here because of Poppy. I came because I shouldn't have told you what I told you. I need you to know that I'll be fine."

"You could talk to Mrs. Silver," Bishop said.

Mrs. Silver was the school counselor–slash–college admissions adviser. Lenore laughed out loud, once, like he'd said something absurd.

"Please. You know what she told Marisol Brooks about her bulimia?"

"I don't want to know about Marisol's bulimia."

"She told her it was all about portion control and positive thinking."

Bishop scrunched his whole face up, squeezing his eyes shut tight before blinking them open again. "I'm not sure I should keep this secret."

"If you tell someone, Mr. Bishop, if you tell my parents or someone from the school, everything will be out of my hands. No way does Headmistress Mackey let a pregnant girl roam the halls, so right away I'm gone from Briarwood, and how does that help me?"

"But your parents—"

"They'll just fight about it. That's what they do. You don't know, Mr. Bishop. Even if, by some miracle, they manage to agree, the whole thing will be about them, the decisions they make. This is nobody's business but mine."

"You made it my business," Bishop said.

"That was a mistake," Lenore said. "That's why I'm here."

Bishop had been teaching long enough to witness plenty of students pretending that everything was under control, that they didn't care about the bad breakup or the failing grade, but he didn't think he'd ever seen a student who had so thoroughly convinced herself that it was true. He was reminded, suddenly, of his own strangeness in this place, isolated by gender and age and by history itself, his narration of the world past tense, when the world Lenore lived in was mostly yet to come.

Pickett scratched the inside of the door.

"Can I pet him?" Lenore said.

Bishop sighed and opened the door, and Pickett came scrabbling out, all tongue and tail, shivering with pent-up excitement, butting his head against Lenore's knees. She pressed her face into the ruff around his neck and raked her fingers down his back.

"He smells like old books," she said.

Lenore held the dog's head in her hands and let him lick her face.

"I'm moving in with Melissa," she told Bishop.

"That's good, I guess. That's something."

Back in the kitchen, when she was gone, Bishop found his soup smoking on the stove, noodles and broth boiled to paste. He gripped the handle with his shirttail and dumped the mess, pot and all, into the trash. His watery drink was waiting on the counter. He drained it, poured another. "Shit," he said, loud enough that Lionel Higgins might have heard. Pickett watched all this with interest. Then, as if it contained some hidden meaning, Bishop listened to his father's message one more time.

Question 4

Eugenia Marsh's second and final play, *Dream Entropy*, opened on January 6, 1979, but ran for only nine performances before being closed, owing to negative reviews and stagnant ticket sales. A particularly scathing assessment was published in the *New York Times*. Which of the following criticisms was/were included in that review?

A) *Dream Entropy* reflects the kind of unabashed navel-gazing and abstraction that gives contemporary theater a bad name.

B) Fine performances can't save this mishmash of memory play and failed postmodern experiment.

C) Ms. Marsh seems to be under the impression that life is little more than an endless loop of ever-repeating history, an idea that might be interesting in theory but which produces very little actual drama when rendered for the stage.

D) All of the above.

XIII

Bishop told people he'd grown up in Richmond, and that was almost true. The home of his childhood could be found in Short Pump, a suburb on the western edge of Richmond proper, so called because of a short-handled pump outside a tavern once located on the carriage route between Richmond and Charlottesville, a place patronized by the likes of Thomas Jefferson and Stonewall Jackson, though there was no sign of that history left to grace Short Pump's present. Whatever it might once have been, the original village was lost to strip malls and shopping centers and planned communities with names like Wythe Station and Graham's Run and Wellesley Landing, names meant to evoke bygone plantations. The more upscale developments were laid out around golf courses or man-made lakes or both.

Bishop's parents did not live in one of these. Their house in Tuckahoe Trace was buried behind so many identical ranchers on so many identical streets that twice in high school, drunk both times, Bishop had pulled into the wrong driveway and been shocked to discover that his key did not open the front door. His memories of the place were so specific, however, so localized—*his* bedroom, *their* kitchen, as opposed to all the duplicate bedrooms and kitchens in all those other houses—that the reality of the place never ceased to amaze him when he returned. The houses really were indistinguishable—bay window on the left, garage on the right—and there were so many of them, hundreds of mailboxes lined up beside hundreds of driveways, each house singled out only by the embellishments beyond its walls: a basketball hoop mounted above a garage, a Marine Corps flag hanging by the door. Given its nature—temporary, prefabricated—Tuckahoe Trace should have been immune to history, but on this Saturday afternoon Bishop steered deeper into the grid wisping vapor trails of memory. Here was the stretch of sidewalk where he'd wrecked his bike, and here was the house where the crazy roller-skating woman lived, and there, no, there, was Haley Polson's window, behind which Bishop had stolen a first kiss in a bedroom identical to his own.

It was almost four o'clock by the time he pulled up to the curb. He let Pickett out and waited for him to relieve himself on the mailbox post before ringing the bell. His father answered the door wearing a bathrobe over a white undershirt and khaki pants. Mercy and Rhett trotted up, but they did not bark or venture out. They peered at Bishop from between his father's legs, his father standing in the doorway with one hand on the knob.

"To what do we owe the pleasure?" he said.

"You called me. You left a message. I thought, you know, I'd drive down instead of just calling back."

"I left you a message? I don't think so. When was that?"

There was an edge of defensiveness in his father's voice.

"Yesterday," Bishop said. "What were you doing home?"

"Mercy's been having kidney problems. If I don't let her out on my lunch break she'll piss up the house."

"Why don't you just leave them in the yard?"

"They're old," his father said.

He was taller than his son, leaner, ropier, the difference in their heights exaggerated by the fact that he was standing on the doorstep while Bishop stood on the ground, stooping to hold Pickett's collar to keep him from bolting through the open door.

"You gonna invite me in?" Bishop said.

His father looked surprised for a second, not displeased but as though the idea hadn't occurred to him until that moment. He shrugged, stepped aside. Bishop turned Pickett loose, and he bounded into Mercy and Rhett, like he'd been launched, and all three dogs went reeling together into the house.

Bishop's mother was stretched out on the couch in the den with an open book propped on her chest, half-moon reading glasses perched on her nose. On TV, volume low, North Carolina was leading Virginia in the ACC basketball tournament. His father let the dogs out into the backyard—all the yards in Tuckahoe Trace were stitched together with chain link—then disappeared into the kitchen.

"We thought you were the Mormons," his mother said. "They keep sending these teenagers to recruit us. You know, your father had people in the Latter-day Saints on his mother's side."

"I didn't know that," Bishop said.

"Well, it's true. They want to bring us back into the ward. It's gotten to where I look forward to their visits. These are nice kids—clean-cut, polite. Your father won't let me answer the door anymore when they come around. He thinks I'm giving them false hope."

"So, no plans to convert?"

"I think not," she said.

The den looked exactly as it had when Bishop went off to college, the same floral-patterned couch and throw pillows, the same prints on the walls—beach scenes mostly, cheaply framed. Bishop's mother loved the beach, and for one week every summer of Bishop's childhood, the family had ferried out to Chincoteague Island, where they had stayed in the same cramped room at the same bed-and-breakfast, a place where there never seemed to be any other kids around. His father swept the sand with a metal detector—once he found a Rolex watch—while Bishop tumbled in the surf. His mother pored through book after book on a towel spread beyond the reach of the tide. They played cards at night or board games in the parlor at the bed-and-breakfast, while older couples sat and watched, mesmerized by Bishop's youth. And somehow all of this seemed to have a restorative effect on Bishop's mother. Now his parents went to Chincoteague without their son, and the prints on the walls were sun-faded, blurry-looking.

Bishop's father returned with a can of beer for Bishop and one for himself. He dropped into his recliner, popped the footrest.

"Well," he said, "what can we do you for?"

"I need a favor."

"Are you in trouble?" his father said.

"What? No, I'm not in trouble."

"It's all right," his mother said. "Whatever it is, we're here to help."

"I need to find somebody. I was hoping Dad could make a call."

"Are they in trouble," his father said, "this person you want to find?"

After all those years with the Department of Corrections, he tended to interact with the world like everybody had committed a crime and it was his job to keep them on the straight and narrow.

"Not that I know of," Bishop said.

"Why are you looking?"

"That's enough of the third degree," his mother said.

Bishop told them about the play and Eugenia Marsh and her connection to Briarwood and his idea to invite her for opening night. He was standing in front of the sliding glass doors, and he felt like he was making a presentation. He could see his shadow stretching toward them on the rug, his hands moving in a way that embarrassed him for some reason.

His mother eyed him for a second, and then she shifted her gaze to her husband, and he lowered the footrest of his recliner and shuffled off to the master bedroom, the location of the only working phone in the house.

When he was gone, his mother said, "I'm glad to see you taking an interest in the arts."

The book was spread open across her chest.

"What are you reading?" Bishop said.

"Oh, some novel. We're getting ready for the spring book sale. They give library employees first dibs on the discards."

"Any good?"

"I haven't made up my mind," his mother said. "It's backwards. Literally. Not only does it begin with the main character's death and move in reverse through his whole life, but tap water rises from the sink and runs up the faucet. Stuff like that. There's a historical angle, something about the Holocaust. You might be interested."

"Backwards?"

"It's thematic," his mother said, "and it is a little show-offy, but I'll tell you what—when you first came in and I stopped reading, everything looked like it was moving in the wrong direction for a second."

The basketball game cut to a commercial for a used-car lot. Then one for a mattress store. In the light through the sliding doors, his mother's skin looked almost translucent. She smiled, conscious of his stare. Though he knew better than most that history was essentially one long obituary for mankind, Bishop was not coping well with his parents' perfectly natural creep toward old age, every instance of forgetfulness a sign of impending dementia, every hint of a limp noted, every stomach bug the beginning of the end. His mother was sixty-six years old, his father three years older, both in excellent health, but Bishop was swamped with melancholy in their presence, as if mourning in advance. He worried that his parents could sense what he was feeling, and he suspected sometimes that they were eager to be rid of him and happier when he was gone.

"Dad called me yesterday," he said.

"He did? What time?"

"I don't know. Lunchtime."

"He comes home to let the dogs out."

"He told me that. He also told me that he didn't remember calling."

"Maybe he didn't call."

"He left a message," Bishop said. "It's on my machine."

"What did he say?"

"He didn't say anything. At least not to me. But I could hear the dogs barking and his voice telling them to hush."

"That sounds like your father." She balanced the book on the back of the couch and swung her legs around. "I should be starting dinner." She pushed through the swinging door into the kitchen. Bishop listened to the cabinets banging open and closed, the faucet running. He could picture her filling the pot, putting water on to boil, fetching pasta from the shelf. He would have bet money she was making spaghetti casserole.

He carried his beer into his old room, across the hall from his parents' room. Everything the same here as well: twin beds, chest of drawers, bookcase filled with paperbacks and model airplanes, Bishop's Rolling Stones poster on the wall, his Redskins pennant. He could picture a younger version of himself in there, reading comic books in bed, a band of light under the door, dirty clothes piled in the corner, but the image was like something he'd seen in a movie about his life. He sipped his beer and looked out the window, his father's voice, deep and muted as his conscience, murmuring over from the master bedroom. Pickett nosed along the fence in the backyard, Mercy and Rhett watching him with their heads cocked, like they couldn't figure what he found so interesting.

Bishop came back into the den just as his mother was emerging from the kitchen. "I hope you'll stay for dinner," she said. Before he could reply, his father returned from the bedroom with Eugenia Marsh's address written on the back of a grocery-store receipt.

"That was quick," Bishop said.

"Ike Rails was on duty this afternoon. You remember Ike Rails." He pointed at the receipt in Bishop's hands. "This Marsh lady has no phone, at least not in her name, not one that Ike could find, but that's the address in her DMV records. If you can believe it, there's a couple of Eugenia Marshes in Virginia, but this is the only one about the right age."

"Thanks, Dad. I owe you."

"It goes without saying that you didn't get that information from me and I most certainly did not get it from Ike Rails."

"He knows that, Frank," his mother said.

Bishop stared at the receipt. *1221 Whiskey Barrel Road, Rockbridge, Virginia*. He flipped it over, as if perhaps the other side might reveal more information, but it was only the litany of his parents' groceries—milk, spaghetti, peanut butter, bread, dog food, lettuce, carrots, salad dressing, coffee, beer—a list so plain and unassuming that reading it raised a lump in Bishop's throat.

After dinner, with Pickett snoozing on the back seat, Bishop drove back to Briarwood in the dark, the miles unfolding without registering, trees blurring past the windows, moonlit fields. All the way home, he kept patting his breast pocket, checking and double-checking that the receipt was still there. He stopped at the gatehouse, and the security guard hit the switch to raise the traffic arm. He motored slowly past the stables and around the curve and up the hill. He had assumed that he'd have to wait until morning to show Coach Fink what he had in his breast pocket, but lights were still burning in her windows. Saturday night. Maybe it wasn't too late. He pulled over in front of her duplex, cut the engine. Pickett roused himself in the back seat, panting hard. For a few minutes, they just sat and watched. Finally, Bishop saw a shadow move past the window, and he left Pickett in the car and made his way to the door. He knocked and waited. Nothing. Tried again.

"Are you there?" he said. "It's Lucas Bishop."

A beat passed before the dead bolt thumped and the door opened, and there was Coach Fink in a Briarwood sweatsuit with her braid loose, hair tumbling down her back and over her shoulders and chest.

"Do you know what time it is?"

"I know. I'm sorry. I've got something to show you."

"It better not be pubes."

"No pubes." He smiled. "This is much better than pubes."

Released from its braid, her hair was crimped and tangled and wild, and Bishop thought she hardly looked like herself.

"Well, all right then," she said. "Let's see what you got."

XIV

Years later, long before Briarwood School for Girls, struggling financially, closed its doors for good rather than open them to boys, at a point in time when Lenore Littlefield was already slightly famous—a pair of indie films, nice notices at Sundance—though not so well known that people recognized her on the street, before her first commercial success, before she met the man who would become her husband, before she abandoned acting altogether for a more private life with this man, still unknown to her, and their children, still unimagined, before her life, in other words, had settled into its true course, and nearly a decade after her days at boarding school, she was wheeling a carry-on through Hartsfield International when she spotted Coach Fink at a nearby gate. The sweatsuit, that braid. Legs crossed like a man's. Running shoes. Definitely her. Coach Fink hadn't noticed Lenore, and Lenore did not call out or change her course—airports were disorienting enough without faces from the past leaping up to greet you—but as she drew closer and then wheeled by, the moment when they might have spoken gone, her memory slipped back to *The Phantom of Thornton Hall*, the last rehearsal before spring break, 1994, that night precisely, for some reason, rather than the performance of the play itself. More specifically she remembered those minutes after rehearsal when Coach Fink gathered the cast in the front row, the point, most nights, when she detailed the many ways they had failed to meet her expectations.

"All right, ladies, listen up. We all know that school lets out for spring break tomorrow. I shouldn't have to remind you that we open two weeks after you get back." She held up the index and middle fingers of her right hand—a peace sign, a shadow-puppet rabbit. "So take your script. Read it on the plane. Read it in the car. Read it on the beach while you're working on your tan. I don't give a damn where you read it. The point is, don't go forgetting everything we've practiced. You've worked too hard. I hope to have something exciting to announce when you return."

And then she did the most surprising thing: she smiled and clapped her hands and sent them on their way, not a single grievance aired. They were terrified by her good mood. As they filed out of the auditorium, bumping shoulders and pushing their arms into their coats, they speculated in nervous murmurs about the sinister nature of Coach Fink's announcement—last-minute changes to the lineup? some kind of performance-enhancing fitness regimen?—but Lenore couldn't help remembering Coach Fink's yearbook picture, the bright mouthful of her dental work.

The dinner bell was clanging when they emerged, girls already clumped on the paths or fanned out across the hill in their nightly migration toward the buffet line and the salad bar. There was something gilded about the night, lit windows glowing in the dining hall and the buildings around the quad. To Lenore the campus looked as dignified and cozy as a village in a movie with a happy ending. She always felt a little spellbound after rehearsal, a little outside herself. It was like being caught up in a trance, except the trance was somehow more real than her real life, as if some other, truer part of herself took control of her faculties and spoke Jenny's lines—until Coach Fink shrilled her whistle and shouted, "Cut," and Lenore blinked and looked around as if shaking off a dream.

Over time footpaths had been worn into the grass, like the trails animals leave through woods and pastures, and as the rest of the cast wandered on toward the dining hall, Lenore peeled away and followed one of these paths in the direction of the library. She found Mrs. Booth at the circulation desk, her glasses hanging around her neck on a delicate silver chain. Mrs. Booth had replaced old Mrs. Pettaway at the beginning of the school year.

"Excuse me," Lenore said. "I was wondering where we keep old copies of the yearbook."

Mrs. Booth was sorting through a stack of checkout tickets and didn't look up as she replied. "Past editions of *The Green and White* are archived in the basement."

"I mean the really old editions," Lenore said. "The yearbooks in the basement stop at 1925."

Mrs. Booth lifted her glasses into place, her eyes suspicious behind the lenses. "Why do you ask?"

"Research," Lenore said.

Mrs. Booth surveyed the room and then waved Lenore around behind the circulation desk and through a locked door into the small, softly lit chamber where the library housed record albums and videocassettes. In addition, Mrs. Booth explained, they also used this space to store printed matter—first editions, antique folios, documents willed to Briarwood by notable alumnae—too valuable or too delicate for public display.

"What are you looking for exactly?" she said, and when Lenore told her, she said, "Ah, a fellow paranormalist, I see." Without having to consider its location, she retrieved the 1917 edition of *The Green and White* from its shelf in a glass-front case. The yearbook was sheathed in some kind of clear plastic. Mrs. Booth opened it to the page and held it up for Lenore. "You may look but you may not touch."

And there she was, Elizabeth Archer, in her Briarwood uniform, hair done up in a French braid, head turned so that the photographer could capture her in three-quarter profile.

"Beautiful, isn't she?" said Mrs. Booth, and Lenore agreed. Her face was too narrow but her eyes were big and dark, and her widow's peak made her look dramatic. It wasn't hard to believe that some boy had loved Elizabeth Archer, and that she had loved him back enough to do herself terrible, terrible harm in Thornton Hall.

Memory is an unpredictable engine, making leaps and creating connections where none are immediately apparent, so there is no way to know for sure why Lenore recalled that night as she moved on through the airport, leaving her old coach behind, that night as opposed to hundreds of other encounters with Coach Fink or any other night, for that matter, in the whole rest of her life, but it occurred to her, as her flight was lifting off, that the last night before spring break marked the final hours of the girl she'd been, the girl she had imagined herself to be, the girl who would become this woman nursing a glass of chardonnay in her window seat and watching city lights fade to pinpricks down below.

That girl had already moved in with Melissa, her dresses and coats hanging in what had been Poppy's closet, her mirror hanging on the wall. That girl remained a mystery to herself. She lay in the dark with her eyes open, headphones cocooning her in sound, images of her family's trip to Disney World playing on the ceiling like home movies. A memory within a memory. She was eight years old. Her father would abandon them before too long. She remembered the garish cartoon elegance of Cinderella Castle, the rocket in Space Mountain careening toward a dead end before veering at the last second, that moment the very essence of relief. She remembered her mother's tennis visor with the pink translucent brim, an accessory she would never admit to owning now. She remembered the sweat in her father's sideburns and how he'd held her in his arms during the nightly fireworks display, despite the fact that she was too big, her toes tapping his shins. She remembered wishing she could live in a place like that forever, all color and music and genial exhaustion.

Melissa was a still and quiet sleeper, hardly moving beneath her covers, hardly breathing, it seemed to Lenore. Removing her headphones and slipping her Walkman under her pillow, Lenore swung out of Poppy's bed and leaned her ear close to Melissa's mouth. She heard no sound, nothing at all like Juliet's apneic rasp, though she could feel faint warm puffs of Melissa's breath against her cheek.

They would have a half day of school tomorrow, a useless day. Melissa's parents lived in Foggy Bottom, and she would give Lenore a ride to DC. Her cover story: she was catching a flight home from Dulles. Once Melissa had dropped her at the airport, Lenore would grab a taxi to some hotel where she could hole up before and after.

When she was certain that Melissa was asleep, she stepped out into the hall and headed up the stairs to her old room. She pushed the door open and stood there for a minute, listening to Juliet snore. As if sensing her presence, Juliet bolted up in bed and clutched her blankets to her throat.

"What do you want?"

"I want," Lenore said, "to talk to the Ouija board."

Juliet stared at her, sagging a little, curious. Under the circumstances, anybody else would have told her to get lost, but Lenore knew that Juliet believed. She was counting on it. Juliet might have been the only girl at Briarwood who understood that sometimes a person needed answers the living couldn't give.

"Light the candle," Juliet said, stretching.

The flame made a luminescent bubble, nudging back the night. Juliet knelt and collected the Ouija board from under her bed. She hesitated, box resting on her thighs.

"You're really good. As Jenny. You can't tell Thessaly I said that."

Lenore sat cross-legged between the beds.

"I won't."

"I just want the play to be great. I want people to remember it and not because we sucked."

"I know."

"And it's better with you as Jenny."

"Thank you," Lenore said.

Juliet unboxed the Ouija board, and they settled their fingers on the planchette, and right away the planchette began to drift, smooth as an air-hockey puck, up to the moon. Juliet stared at Lenore, tiny candle flames reflected in her eyes.

"Looks like you're not the only one who wants to talk."

"So what do we do?" Lenore said.

"You came up here with questions. Ask. And try to keep it simple. It's better if the spirits can answer yes or no."

Lenore closed her eyes. She could feel her pulse jumping in her throat.

"Are you happy?" she said.

The planchette skidded smoothly up to *no* but paused only for a moment, like a rolling stop, before continuing on to *yes*.

"I think that means the answer is unclear," Juliet said, "like a maybe."

Lenore nodded. That sounded right.

"Is happiness possible?" she asked the Ouija board, and the planchette repeated the same course—*no*, then *yes*.

"Are you alone?"

No, then *yes*.

"Do you remember your life?"

No, then *yes*.

"Do you know who I am?"

A simple *yes* this time.

"Do you know why I wanted to talk to you?"

Yes again.

"Will I be happy?"

No, then *yes*, and through all this Juliet was quiet, her fingers along for the ride as the planchette skated across the board. And all those years later, sleep settling over her on the plane, Lenore could not be certain if every detail of her memory was accurate, but the images flashing through her mind seemed real enough, and the spirits hadn't told her anything she hadn't already understood—there were no easy answers. Finally, as Lenore was winding down, Juliet said, "I've got a question. Does Coach Fink know it was me who left the envelope on her doorstep?"

Lenore had no idea what she was talking about but the spirits did.

No, then *yes*.

XV

Coach Fink insisted on driving. She had her reasons. She told herself that Bishop's car was in sorry shape, the windshield fractured by a long, diagonal crack, the tires half bald, the engine rattling like pebbles in a can. You could hear him coming from all the way down at the gatehouse. Lord knows how long it had been since he'd changed his oil or his antifreeze. Coach Fink, on the other hand, was meticulous about her fluids and had her tires rotated every three thousand miles. On top of that, Bishop refused to leave his dog behind. Coach Fink liked dogs just fine, but she had no desire to be cooped up for six hours round-trip with Pickett's hot breath on her neck. Dogs belonged in the backs of pickup trucks. That's another thing she told herself. And these reasons were not false, not really, but there was more to her insistence than she was willing to admit. From the moment Bishop appeared on her doorstep with Eugenia Marsh's address in his breast pocket, Coach Fink had allowed herself to be swept along on the wave of his enthusiasm, uncharacteristic to say the least and grounds enough for hesitation. His interest puzzled her, but she was touched by his concern and grateful for his help, even if she was beginning to have her doubts about his plan. Say they managed to find Eugenia Marsh and say they somehow convinced her to show up for opening night—would the prospect of her presence render the cast more talented? Grant Coach Fink new insight into the production? The closer they got to the hour of departure, the more she worried that courting Eugenia Marsh was less an opportunity to shine than a recipe for public humiliation. Driving was a means of reasserting her control.

Despite her questions and her misgivings, she steered them south on Lee Highway, a vein of optimism still pulsing through her. She wanted to believe that Bishop was right, that something positive might come of this. She'd nearly tipped her hand to the cast at their last rehearsal, but she'd restrained herself and she was glad. Odds were Eugenia Marsh would send them packing, but as the road unspooled beneath them, a smudge of daytime moon visible above the trees, Coach Fink couldn't shake the feeling that she'd been rushing toward this morning ever since Headmistress Mackey assigned her to the Drama Club.

Lee Highway was mostly four-lane, rural, paralleled by power lines, but periodically it narrowed as they navigated some small town—Warrenton, Bealeton, Culpeper. Fast-food franchises and bank branches. Tanning salons everywhere.

Bishop sighed and cleared his throat.

"The biggest cavalry battle in American history took place just up the road. The Battle of Brandy Station. Seventeen thousand mounted soldiers. All those sabers in the morning light and the sound of all those charging horses. Can you imagine? It must have been incredible."

Pickett had never ridden in the back of a truck, so as a precaution Bishop had clipped a leash to the dog's collar and run it through the sliding window into the cab, the other end looped around his wrist. As Pickett wandered in the bed, the leash occasionally lifted Bishop's arm and lowered it again like a puppet's, and Coach Fink had to grit her teeth to keep from pointing out the idiocy of this arrangement.

"Who won?" she said.

"Depends on who you ask. The actual fighting was back and forth, and technically the Federals withdrew, but the battle marked the end of the Confederate cavalry's dominance in the East. If you put a gun to my head and forced me to pick a winner, I'd have to go with Jeb Stuart and the rebs, but it was a moral victory for the Union."

"I don't put much stock in moral victories."

History held no interest for Coach Fink. She did not like to consider other people's lives any more than she liked to think about her own. This was one of the reasons she appreciated sports. Whereas many coaches taught sports as a metaphor for life, Coach Fink admired the beauty of their limited application. You subjugated yourself to the team and dedicated yourself to a single game, a single moment, even—this free throw or that sideline hit—and when it was over you put the game or the moment behind you because the next one was already bearing down. Yes, it was important to learn from past mistakes, but it was equally important not to dwell on them.

In Charlottesville, they merged onto I-64, which carried them over Afton Mountain, with its scenic-view pull-offs, and then down through Waynesboro behind a yellow Porsche with a vanity license plate, LASTTOY. Stray white houses dotted the landscape, TV antennae snagging signals from the air. Pale light shone on the trees and the fences and the horses grazing in the fields. Bishop's arm went up on the end of the leash and hung there like a conductor paused in that moment before he gestured the orchestra to begin. Coach Fink couldn't stand it anymore.

"What do you think will happen if he jumps?" she said.

"I don't think he will," Bishop said. "Are you trying to freak me out?"

"If he jumps, that leash will break your arm and his neck both."

Bishop hesitated before reeling Pickett in and unclipping the hook from his collar. Pickett tried to poke his head into the cab, but Coach Fink nudged him back with her elbow and slid the window shut. She worried she'd hurt Bishop's feelings about the leash. He kept swiveling around to check on Pickett, but the dog was fine. She could see him in the rearview, ears flapping in the wind.

"You know these are my old stomping grounds," she said, steering them onto the I-81 ramp and merging into a new stream of traffic, nothing but long-haul trucks all of a sudden—freezer trucks and tankers and flatbeds bearing big pieces of machinery and livestock trailers with vented sides and plenty of your standard eighteen-wheelers—everything a country might want en route through Virginia. "My parents ran a summer camp near Clifton Forge."

"How'd you wind up at Briarwood?"

"The camp was all boys." Coach Fink shrugged. "And I have three older brothers. My folks thought I needed a more feminine influence."

"I can picture it," Bishop said. "You shooting hoops and playing baseball with the boys. Archery and horseback riding. Canoeing. What else do they have at summer camp?"

"That's about it. There was a pool, I guess."

"Maybe we could stop by on the way back. I'd like to see it."

"They went belly-up in '83. My dad put a shotgun in his mouth. My mom remarried and moved to Hershey, Pennsylvania."

"Jesus," Bishop said. "I'm sorry."

"It's just what happened," Coach Fink said. "After Briarwood, I attended the University of Delaware on a basketball scholarship."

They arrived in Rockbridge County just shy of one o'clock. Bishop had a map of Virginia open on his lap. This got them as far as the exit but no farther. He wanted to stop for directions at the first gas station they passed, but Coach Fink pressed on. Same at the second gas station. She did not explain herself. She was trusting some inner compass. She kept driving like she knew where she was going. Finally, maybe ten miles from the interstate, they arrived at Mother's Best Country Store, and she pulled into the lot. The store looked more like a small house with a tin roof and a front porch than a place of business. Coach Fink planted her sneakers on the ground and twisted her hips from side to side.

"I feel like I've been here before," she said.

While Bishop walked Pickett off into the grass, Coach Fink went inside behind the jangling of a bell. There was no one at the counter, but there were jars of pickled eggs and pickled pigs' feet and a bubbling Crock-Pot filled with cocktail sausages. The air smelled of vinegar and dust. Under the windows hunched a waist-high antique Royal Crown cooler with a black cat perched upon the lid.

"Hello?" Coach Fink said.

After a minute, a door opened at the back of the store, and an old woman poked her head in, her arms filled with laundry. "Give me a sec. I couldn't hear the bell over the washing machine."

She ducked out of sight again, and Coach Fink perused the merchandise on the rows of shelves—sacks of white bread and cans of tomato soup and tins of deviled ham. Everything looked like it had been there for a while. The woman returned and took her place on a stool behind the register. She was wearing a faded pink housedress, her long gray hair caught up in a frazzled bun.

"How can I help you?"

"We're looking for Whiskey Barrel Road," Coach Fink said. "I was hoping you might give us some directions."

"You gonna buy something?"

Coach Fink bristled but restrained herself. "Do you keep bottled water in the cooler? I didn't want to disturb your cat."

"That's not my cat, and no, we don't, just soda and ice cream sandwiches. There's a spigot outside if you want water."

Coach Fink pressed her lips together. She could feel the muscles in her neck bunching into knots. Without paying much attention, she selected a package of pork rinds from the shelf. She paid, waited.

"Whiskey Barrel Road?" she said.

"Never heard of it."

"I'm sorry?"

"I said I never heard of Whiskey Barrel Road."

"You acted like if I bought something you'd give me directions."

"I did no such thing."

"I'm telling you that's what happened," Coach Fink said, "and I'll tell you something else. I think you know exactly how to find Whiskey Barrel Road but you're holding out on me for some reason."

"You can think whatever you want," the woman said.

"Lady, I'm warning you. I am here on what will probably turn out to be a fool's errand, and I'm not sure how I feel about that, and I strongly advise you to come clean ASAP."

At that moment, in the tense and hovering silence, Bishop entered, wiping his feet. "I could go for some beef jerky," he said, and then he stopped and looked around. "Is there a problem?"

"There's about to be if this old lady doesn't tell me how to find Whiskey Barrel Road."

"Have you tried asking politely?"

The woman behind the register glared defiantly at Coach Fink. "There's only one reason anybody ever comes around here asking after Whiskey Barrel Road."

"We're looking for a playwright named Eugenia Marsh," Bishop said.

"That's the reason."

"I knew you were holding out on me," Coach Fink said.

"We had reporters sniffing around the last few weeks, but you two don't look like reporters. My guess is you're just crazy fans. That play must really be something, the way you people show up here all the time."

"I am not a fan," Coach Fink said, "and you have about ten seconds before bad things begin to happen in this dump."

"Let's everybody take it easy," Bishop said.

Coach Fink wondered what she would do if the old woman refused to answer, if her threats and posturing yielded no results. Part of her wanted to find out. She thought she might tip that jar of pickled eggs onto the floor. She pictured shattered glass, soggy eggs rolling around, pinkish fluid spreading across the hardwood planks.

"I hate that goddamn play," she said.

The obvious truth of this remark, combined with a note of hopelessness in Coach Fink's voice, had the effect of letting the air out of the situation. Turned out the old woman had no reason to protect Eugenia Marsh. She just enjoyed having a secret almost as much as she disliked strangers. While the old woman wrote directions on the back of Bishop's map, she admitted that Eugenia Marsh was a bit of a snob when you got right down to it, the kind of person who could live in a place for decades and spend a grand total of fifty bucks or so in another person's country store.

They followed her directions for a few miles down Route 16, then made a right on Sour Mash Lane and a left on Whiskey Barrel Road. The sign was so overgrown with ivy that they passed it twice before Bishop noticed it tangled in the greenery. "Must have been a distillery around here," he said, and Coach Fink felt about his comment the way she often felt about history as a subject—it was engaged in pointing out the obvious. Human beings existed in the past. Events occurred at this location. Well, no shit, Coach Fink thought. And yet, as she piloted them down Whiskey Barrel Road, ivy climbing the pines and the bear oaks and draping tendrils from the highest branches, these tendrils dangling low enough in places to brush the windshield of her truck, she felt the presence of history in a way she couldn't have explained, this feeling akin to but not exactly like déjà vu. Dapples of shadow on the pavement seemed infused with the uncanny; clouds wisped across the sky in arcane patterns. They passed a dilapidated barn on Bishop's side of the road, the roof caved in, the rest of the structure leaning hard but hanging on, the barn, too, threaded through with vines, as if ivy was the only thing holding it up. Eventually a split-rail fence took shape in the undergrowth, and the ivy began to thin, creeping along the fence for a while before falling away to reveal fields of hay grass and, in the distance, the blunt and hazy shape of the Blue Ridge Mountains shouldering up beyond a line of trees.

And then a house stranded in a field—white clapboard, green shutters. Boxwoods planted around the porch. Chimneys on both sides. A pea-gravel drive dwindling toward the house through a row of cedars. Not identical to the house in Coach Fink's dream but close enough to make her cheeks go hot, her hands numb on the wheel. There was a mailbox on a fence post down by the road, and Coach Fink braked to look inside.

Empty but for an old bird's nest.

"What're you doing?" Bishop said.

"Nothing," Coach Fink said. "Just making sure we're in the right place."

"The address is on the mailbox."

She turned into the driveway, tires crunching on the gravel, Pickett pacing in the bed, and stopped in front of the house. No other cars in sight.

"Tell me again—why didn't we just write a letter?"

"Letters take too long," Bishop said, "and are too easily ignored."

"Looks like nobody's home," she said.

Coach Fink stayed in the truck while Bishop climbed the porch steps and knocked on the door. He waited with his hands in his pockets. Pickett whined but he stayed put. A wind chime played softly in the breeze, the sound of it blending in her ears with Pickett's whine. After a minute, Bishop came down the steps and dropped the tailgate for Pickett. "We'll check around the back," he said, and she watched him peeking in the windows as he went, cupping his hands around his eyes, Pickett whizzing on the boxwoods. They disappeared behind the house, and when they reemerged on the other side, she opened her door and stepped out into the gravel.

"Let's wait awhile," Bishop said.

He found a branch under the trees and tossed it into the field for Pickett. The dog bounded through the hay grass, leaping high, then vanishing, only his tail visible, then leaping into sight again. Coach Fink sat on the tailgate of her truck. Pickett found the branch and brought it back and Bishop let it fly again. They waited more than an hour, a breeze washing over the field like wind over the sea.

XVI

It was Bishop's idea to stay the night. They found rooms at the Rebel Rest Motel out by the interstate. For some reason, the manager booked them on separate floors, Coach Fink at ground level, her pickup parked just outside her door, Bishop on the second and highest floor, the view from his window an equally vacant chain motel across the road. He filled a plastic ice bucket with water for Pickett and left the TV on the news so the dog wouldn't get lonely while he and Coach Fink drove into the town of Lexington to find a place to eat.

Like Briarwood, the nearby college was on spring break, and life seemed on hold without the students. Just two cars parked on Main Street, a brown Volvo hatchback and an old blue Mercedes, its left taillight busted out. Quiet brick storefronts: the coffee shop, the used bookstore, the hardware store, the haberdashery. The college was named for George Washington and Robert E. Lee, but the town seemed to favor Lee. A mannequin in the window of the haberdashery sported a bow tie with a Confederate flag motif. This was not to mention their motel. Perhaps the old Confederate felt more a part of the place than the revolutionary because Lee had actually lived here for a while, serving as president of the college after the Civil War, whereas Washington had only provided an endowment. Bishop had always thought Lee an odd exemplar for the Southern male—meditative and spiritual by nature, physically unimpressive, more pastor than warrior by most accounts. Plus, Lee failed in his great campaign, whereas Washington, also a Virginian, was remembered for chopping down cherry trees and wintering at Valley Forge and routing Cornwallis at Yorktown. He supposed George Washington belonged to national history while Lee was mired in the history of the South. All of this Bishop considered over slices of pepperoni and mushroom in a red leatherette booth at a place called Small Paul's Pizzeria.

"I love a college town when the students are away," he said around a mouthful. "You get all the good without the bad."

"So in this equation students are the bad?"

"You have to admit they make a lot of unnecessary racket."

They had a pitcher of beer and shakers of powdered Parmesan and red pepper flakes. The jukebox played a song by Johnny Cash. Just finding Eugenia Marsh's house seemed like progress.

Coach Fink sipped her beer, wiping foam from her lip with the back of her hand. As if patching into Bishop's line of thought, she said, "You think she'll be home in the morning?"

"I have a good feeling," Bishop said.

On the way back to the Rebel Rest, they stopped at a convenience store for supplies—toothbrushes and toothpaste, shaving cream and disposable razors. Coach Fink bought a Twinkie for dessert. Bishop added a can of dog food and a six-pack. He took Pickett for walk around the motel parking lot and iced the beer in the bathroom sink, and then it dawned on him that he had no way to open the dog-food can. He tried the front desk, but the night clerk was no help, so he headed for Coach Fink's room. Her window looked out over the sidewalk, and she'd left the curtains open. He could see her inside doing sit-ups on the floor with her feet wedged under the dresser. Eyes closed, fingers linked behind her head. Still in her street clothes—jeans and a flannel shirt. Blue light from the TV played across her face. She touched one elbow to her knee and then the other, and Bishop didn't know whether to knock or leave her be. He stepped away from the window and counted to a hundred with his back to the door, but when he looked again she was going strong. The tendons in her neck put him in mind of guy wires on a bridge. He was still watching when she stopped and opened her eyes and saw him standing there. She made a face and rolled to her feet.

"I should have figured you for a perv," she said, cracking the door.

Bishop showed her the dog food.

"You don't by any chance have a way to open a can?"

Coach Fink sighed and pushed past him to her truck. She kept a Swiss Army knife in the glove compartment and managed to pry up one side of the lid. On TV, a young Sissy Spacek was cowering in a shower stall, being pelted with tampons by her schoolmates because her period had arrived and she didn't know what it was.

"Is that *Carrie*?" Bishop said

"It had just started when I caught you sneaking a peek," Coach Fink said. "You're welcome to join me."

Bishop said, "I'll grab some beers."

Back in his room, Bishop used his fingers to scoop the dog food out for Pickett. He washed his hands and sat at a small table by the window while Pickett ate. He'd been trying not to think about Lenore, but an image of her flared up against his will. She was staring out the window of his classroom—bored by history, distracted by the unbearable complications of the present. The obvious advantage of history is hindsight, but even so, people kept on making the same mistakes. Nobody ever learned. Nobody ever knew what was right or what was true. Not for sure, not in the present. He carried the beer downstairs with Pickett at his side. Coach Fink had left the door ajar, and Pickett trotted into her room like he expected to be welcomed. Coach Fink was propped on a nest of pillows in one of two double beds. She patted the mattress, and Pickett hopped up beside her.

"I used to have a dog," she said.

Bishop passed Coach Fink a beer and took his place on the empty bed.

"Her name was Shirley," Coach Fink said. "A Shetland sheepdog. She liked to herd the neighbor's cows."

Now a vision of young Coach Fink floated into his mind, a little girl in jeans and sneakers shooting hoops at a basketball goal nailed to the side of a barn, a Shetland sheepdog dancing around her legs. The vision was probably bogus, cribbed from some nostalgic G-rated portrayal of rural life. He had a hard time picturing her as a Briarwood student, though he knew she had been. On TV, Bible in hand, Piper Laurie was berating Sissy Spacek, mother hectoring daughter on the evils of lust and fornication. Bishop pointed.

"I bused her table once. Sissy Spacek. I used to work at this place called Faulkner's back in undergrad. She lives just outside Charlottesville. Came in with her husband. They had the crab cakes, as I recall."

"You can't throw a rock without hitting a celebrity anymore," Coach Fink said. "I saw Robert Duvall one time at a gas station in Loudoun County. He was just standing there at the pumps like everybody else."

Bishop remembered how the actress's presence among the ordinary diners had done nothing to make her seem more real. Instead, the restaurant itself had taken on the sheen of something imagined.

"Anyhow," he said. "She's pretty great in *The Phantom of Thornton Hall*."

Coach Fink pushed up on her elbows.

"What're you talking about?"

"The PBS thing," Bishop said. "Sissy Spacek was great."

"There's a damn movie?" Coach Fink said.

"Well, it's public television not Hollywood but yeah. Recorded live on Broadway after it won the Pulitzer."

"How come nobody told me?"

"I assumed you'd seen it. I got it from the school library. Sissy Spacek plays Jenny. I forget who plays Eleanor, but you'd recognize her if you saw her. She's on a soap commercial now."

Coach Fink huffed and crossed her ankles. Bishop looked over at her, but her face was hidden from view by the table lamp. He could see her left hand opening and closing on the blanket. With her right hand, she balanced the beer can on the flat plain of her stomach.

"What're we doing here, Bishop?" she said. "What're *you* doing here?"

"That's complicated," Bishop said.

Coach Fink swung her legs around and stood between the beds with her hands on her hips. Glaring at him. She looked furious, dangerous. She toed her sneakers off. Then she lunged toward the edge of the bed, grabbed Bishop by the ears, and kissed him. Her lips were chapped. His eyes were open. Her freckles blurred. She pulled away and held his gaze. "You know what I like about this movie?" she said, jerking a thumb over her shoulder at the TV. A pause stretched out between them, long enough that Bishop began to worry that she wanted him to guess, but after a moment she provided the answer to her question. "The freak wins."

"That's not how I remember it," Bishop said.

She kissed him again, and this time he kissed her back, his hands on her ribs, her shoulders. He let her unbuckle his belt, then lifted his hips to tug his jeans down while she stepped out of hers. They kissed again. Coach Fink took him in her fist and squeezed until he swelled. She straddled him, aiming him with her fingers. She pressed her face into his neck and found her rhythm. Breath hissed between her teeth and behind that, he could hear Sissy Spacek making her case to Piper Laurie. "I've been invited to the prom," she said. Before long would come the pig's blood and the fire and the hand grasping up from the grave. The way Bishop remembered it, that movie turned out badly for everyone involved.

* * *

Later, because they were feeling restless and awkward, because they'd finished Bishop's beer and the movie was over and they could think of nothing else to do, they drove back out to Whiskey Barrel Road. Coach Fink cut the headlights and parked her truck beside the mailbox. There was a car in the driveway, windshield catching moonlight, but Bishop convinced Coach Fink they'd have better luck in the morning. Pickett sniffed at the air, thrilled by this strange outing, the house a silhouette of its daytime self, stars scattered across the night like beads from a broken strand of pearls.

"You'd have to really want to be alone," Coach Fink said, "to live in a place like this all by yourself."

"I get the impression that she didn't like being famous very much."

"Is that why she quit writing?"

Bishop shrugged in the dark. "Her second play tanked. She had some personal problems. Nobody knows but her, I guess. Maybe she just didn't have anything else to say."

Pickett circled, then settled on his belly. The dashboard clock glowed 11:58. Without looking at him, Coach Fink said, "I should tell you that we probably won't be doing that again. The sex, I mean."

"I appreciate your honesty," Bishop said.

"I don't mean to hurt your feelings. It was nice and all."

"I'm glad you liked it."

"Well, I did," she said, "but I feel like we should make that more of a onetime thing." She turned to face him, both hands on the wheel. "This is the part where you tell me you liked it, too."

"I liked it, too," he said.

They sat there watching the house without speaking for what seemed to Bishop like a long time, but the silence between them was not uncomfortable. Finally, Coach Fink reached for the keys and drove them back to the motel, where they retired to their separate rooms.

In the morning, at the house on Whiskey Barrel Road, they found Eugenia Marsh up on an extension ladder cleaning her gutters, an old blue Mercedes out front, the one from Main Street with the busted taillight. She was wearing overalls, a long-johns top, yellow rubber dish gloves. She didn't acknowledge the sound of Coach Fink's tires on the gravel, just kept tossing sticks and leaves over her shoulder. Her hair cut in that familiar bob.

"Is that her?" Coach Fink said.

"Must be."

"I can't believe we found her," Coach Fink said, and Bishop felt a sudden billow of pride.

He stepped out of the truck, and a moment later Coach Fink did the same. The doors thumped shut. Still no response from Eugenia Marsh. They cast uneasy glances at each other across the hood. There was an intensity to the woman's focus that made Bishop hesitant to speak. He was trying to think of a delicate way to break the silence, when Eugenia Marsh said, "There's not a tree within thirty feet of the house but somehow every winter the gutters clog up with detritus. Judging by the volume of acorns, my money's on squirrels. They must be nesting up here, the little buggers."

She climbed down from the ladder and removed the glove from her right hand, tugging first at her fingertips, then peeling forward from the wrist, remarkably elegant for such a simple gesture. She introduced herself to Coach Fink and then to Bishop, shaking hands with each in turn.

"We're sorry to just show up like this," Bishop said.

"It's no bother."

Bishop knew her face from the photograph in the newspaper. The circles beneath her eyes had darkened and her skin had roughened over the years. It was disorienting to see those eyes in person, like recognizing a movie star on the street or spotting someone you know on the TV news. Herself and not herself.

Coach Fink said, "The lady at Mother's Best told us you had crazy fans hassling you all the time. I want to be clear that we're not fans."

Eugenia Marsh laughed. "You don't appreciate my work?"

"That's not what she meant," Bishop said.

"I'm only teasing. Doris exaggerates. I get maybe one fan a year, and to be honest, their visits are not unwelcome. They're graduate students mostly. It's nice to know that you're remembered, even if there was a time when I would rather have been forgotten." While she spoke, she walked over to the truck and lifted on her toes to scratch Pickett's head. "You're a handsome dog. Would you like a bowl of water?"

"What I meant," Coach Fink said, "is we're not crazy. We want to invite you to come see your play. We're doing *The Phantom of Thornton Hall* at Briarwood, and we open in three weeks."

"Why don't you fix him some water?" Eugenia Marsh pointed at Coach Fink. "This handsome fellow looks thirsty. You should find a bowl under the kitchen sink."

Coach Fink scowled but trotted up the steps and into the house. Eugenia Marsh lowered the tailgate, and Pickett jumped down and sniffed her ankles. She smiled, climbing the extension ladder with her eyes. "It never ends, does it? We're always a step behind in life. As soon as you finish a task a new one needs doing."

"I know what you mean," Bishop said.

"Is Augusta Mackey still at Briarwood? If memory serves, she was promoted to headmistress after I graduated."

"She's still there, still going strong."

"I used to wonder if that woman had magical powers."

"She does give that impression."

"It's hard to believe Augusta Mackey has approved a performance of *The Phantom of Thornton Hall*. We didn't get along so well when I was a student."

"I think everyone was a little bit surprised."

Coach Fink appeared empty-handed on the porch. Over the house, the sky ranged wide and empty.

"There's no bowl under the sink," she said.

"Try the cabinet next to the refrigerator," said Eugenia Marsh. "I'm picturing a big aluminum mixing bowl."

When Coach Fink was out of sight of again, Bishop said, "I should probably let her tell you—she's the one directing the play—but she's been having trouble with the cast. Knowing you were going to be in the audience, that would give them a little incentive, something to get excited about, something to work for."

"And how do you fit in?"

Bishop hesitated. "I teach history," he said. "I thought you might be interested to know that Briarwood has accepted money from Disney for a new computer lab."

"That sounds just like Augusta Mackey. Always the pragmatist. She believes she's picked the winning side."

"I was hoping you might have something to say about that."

"I might," said Eugenia Marsh, "but I don't make public appearances. You know that or you wouldn't have come out here looking for me."

"There's something else," Bishop said.

"There always is."

He reminded himself that he hadn't promised Lenore. She'd insisted, but he'd never agreed.

"The lead in the play," he said, "the girl who's playing Jenny, she's pregnant. I'm pretty sure I'm the only one she's told."

Slowly, Eugenia Marsh swiveled her head to look at him more directly, as if she hadn't quite taken him in before, and he had the sense that she was looking through him, not into him exactly but at something behind him, beyond him. "Have you read my second play?" she said. Bishop admitted that he had not, but she just kept staring until Coach Fink returned and set the bowl of water at the foot of the steps.

"I guess Bishop's already given you the scoop?"

Pickett drank deep and wagged his tail.

Eugenia Marsh said, "More or less."

"I've been having this dream," Coach Fink said, "where I'm waiting for a letter that never comes. Or sometimes it comes, but I can't get to the mailbox. I think the dream is about you somehow."

Eugenia Marsh pushed her hand into the dish glove and started for the ladder. "I must tell you that this is certainly the most intriguing visit I've had in quite some time." She paused halfway up, looked back over her shoulder. "I appreciate your invitation, and you have my word that I will give it serious consideration. Please tell the cast for me that it's vital to hold something back. Keep the mystery right behind you. Make the audience do a little work. That's especially important in *The Phantom of Thornton Hall*."

"I don't know what that means," Coach Fink said.

"If you like, you're welcome to poke around inside. The graduate students who come never seem to believe that I've quit writing. They imagine that I'm hiding a dozen plays under the bed."

After a moment, to be polite, Bishop walked up the steps and stood in the front room—it would have been called the parlor back when this house was built—wondering what he was meant to see. The furniture was all wrong, he thought, glass and chrome and black-and-white photographs of glamorous-looking people, leftovers from her past, where country antiques would have been a better fit. She wasn't going to come for opening night. She was just humoring them. Out of curiosity, he wandered down the hall looking for her bedroom. The door was open, end tables littered with loose change and mail, mostly catalogues for seed and lingerie. Bishop knelt, just to be sure, and peeked under the bed.

XVII

Lenore paid cash up front for eight nights at the Marriott in a room with two queen beds and a view of the Washington Monument. She registered as Jenny March. She didn't have to think about it. She just filled out the form. Nobody asked questions. As Jenny March, she glided up the elevator and keyed open her room. She turned on the TV with the remote and perused the on-demand movies. She stood at the window with one hand pressed against the cold glass. *Obelisk*, she thought, a bit of art history vocab swimming to the surface of her mind. A tall, four-sided monument tapering to a pyramid-like point. Famous examples could be found in Paris, Istanbul, and right here in our nation's capital.

Her appointment wasn't until Monday, so she had the whole weekend to kill, and the hotel had put a bigger crimp in her budget than she'd anticipated. Mostly, she just walked. She lapped the National Mall, past the museums and the monuments, everything cast in the same colorless granite. She hoofed up Pennsylvania Avenue to the White House, tourists snapping photos through the fence. The weather wasn't great, but she bought a cheap umbrella from a vendor's cart. She kept moving through the rain as if some part of her understood that fear and gloom would overtake her if she stopped.

On Sunday, she looped the reflecting pool, damp cherry blossoms littering the path. The rain fell so softly she had to squint to see it, but she could feel it on her cheeks and on her hands. More an idea of rain than actual rain. Just past the Washington Monument, she was overtaken by a group of schoolchildren, dozens of them swarming past in noisy clumps and fluid bunches, chaperones hustling to keep everyone in line. There was no order to the way they moved or the sounds they made, that pure and joyful racket. Even the reprimands of the chaperones sounded more amused than harried. Lenore followed the group up a flight of stone steps and through a revolving door, and suddenly she was standing in the Museum of American History, voices and footsteps echoing off the marble floors. The chaperones gathered the kids for a head count, and Lenore ducked into the nearest exhibit. Mounted behind a wall of glass was an enormous American flag, the very flag that had inspired the national anthem, the honest-to-God star-spangled banner. Tattered. Shot through with holes. Informational plaques were situated all over the place, but Lenore didn't read them. She knew the basics from Mr. Bishop's class: the War of 1812, Baltimore Harbor, Francis Scott Key. Dim light. Faint music. Fifteen stars, one of them poked out by what must have been a cannonball. Lenore wondered which state was represented by the missing star. She kept waiting to feel moved or inspired, but nothing came. Disney would have done it better, she thought. Disney would have made her feel something, even if it was sentimental and half-true.

So Lenore walked on, slogging all the way to the east end of the Mall, past the familiar dome of the Capitol building and five more blocks to Union Station, where she called Poppy's home number collect from a bank of pay phones on the wall.

"My dad is gonna kill me for accepting the charges."

"Oh my God. Poppy? Is that really you? We've been calling but your mother always answers."

"I know. They've got me in full lockdown. But they're out for a couple of hours. They do brunch every Sunday after church."

"We miss you," Lenore said.

"I figured you would have forgotten me by now."

"Don't be stupid. Everybody is wearing black armbands. An underground movement has sprung up among the freshmen. They call themselves the Red Hand, and they're dedicated to—I don't know what they're dedicated to."

Poppy laughed. "The Red Hand? Where'd that come from?"

"Didn't we study the Red Hand in Mr. Bishop's class? It sounded right."

"I think you mean the Black Hand. From World War I."

"Whatever," Lenore said.

"Where are you?" Poppy said. "It's noisy."

Lenore mashed the phone against her ear.

"I'm at a pay phone," she said, hoping Poppy wouldn't press.

"Have you moved in with Melissa?"

"Last week."

"I'm glad," Poppy said. "I hate to think of you still stranded up there with Juliet Demarinis."

"She's not so bad."

"Since when?"

"I don't know. We're in the play and everything."

"How's that going?"

"Fine. Better, I guess."

"I want to see it," Poppy said. "I've been hassling my mom about letting me come for opening night, but so far she hasn't budged."

"You can't really blame her," Lenore said.

"No, but it would piss off Headmistress Mackey if I showed up. You know what I should do? I should run away from home. I should return to Briarwood in secret, bent on sabotage and revenge. I should unleash the mighty forces of the Red Hand."

"Don't do that," Lenore said.

"I probably won't."

After they hung up, she sat on a bench and watched the people hurrying to catch their trains. Parents with children. Businessmen in their suits. Ladies with shopping bags over their arms. Bums. Soldiers. Nuns. She just watched. She thought that if she sat there long enough every single American might pass before her eyes.

The rain blew over Sunday night, leaving the sky a smoggy blue. Lenore walked up Pennsylvania Avenue to E Street. The clinic wasn't hard to find. The protesters were a giveaway, not too many, six or seven older women and a girl who looked about Lenore's age, holding a sign that said *Abortion = Bloody Murder* on one side and *A Moral Wrong*

Should Not Be a Constitutional Right on the other. She'd clearly spent more time on the *Bloody Murder* side. The background was shaded black, the letters red and dripping, as if oozing blood, whereas the *Moral Wrong* side had been scribbled in a hurry, sloppy, no embellishment at all. Lenore stood on the sidewalk next to the girl.

"You been out here long?" she said.

"Just since they opened. Not a lot of action yet."

The clinic occupied a tan brick building across the street. The windows were frosted so you couldn't see in from the outside, but it wasn't at all the cheerless shambles Lenore had expected. The frosted windows gave the building a modern and businesslike air. The only suggestion of the unusual was a security guard posted beside the door.

"What happens when somebody shows up?"

"That's when we start chanting."

"What do you chant?"

"Oh, we usually just spell *life* like cheerleaders—gimme an *L*, gimme an *I*, gimme an *F* . . ." Her voice trailed off.

"Gimme an *E*?" Lenore suggested.

"I thought that was implied."

Lenore smiled despite herself. "How come you're not in school?"

"I'm homeschooled." The girl pointed at a woman in a Virginia Tech Hokies sweatshirt pouring coffee from a thermos into a Styrofoam cup. "That's my mom."

The other women in the group were sitting on folding chairs, playing cards on the lid of a blue ice chest. Beneath the lid, Lenore guessed, were cans of Coke and egg-salad sandwiches and sliced apples, all the supplies they would need for a long day of protesting. There were more signs in a stack on the sidewalk, at least three times as many signs as there were protesters. The sign on top of the stack read *Rescue those being led away to death, Pr. 24:11* in neatly stenciled letters. Lenore didn't recognize the quote. She couldn't even remember if her mother kept a Bible in the house. She imagined the women swapping out signs like fresh ammunition.

"How about you?" the girl said.

"I'm on spring break."

"That's cool." The girl held out her hand. "I'm Bliss."

"Jenny," Lenore said, and they shook.

"You here to see the sights?"

"Something like that."

Bliss lifted the sign from her shoulder, spun it around a few times, then let it rest again.

"You should check out the Air and Space Museum. The planetarium movie is pretty awesome."

"I will," Lenore said.

They stood there watching the clinic. A city bus rumbled by. A pigeon landed and pecked at something in the street.

"Go ahead," Bliss said. "I'll give you a head start."

"Do what?"

Bliss tipped her chin toward the clinic. "Make a run for it. I'll let you get halfway before I start the chant."

Lenore might have walked away if she'd had somewhere else to go. Instead she took a breath and stepped into the street, a little wobbly, as if wading into a swiftly moving stream. The pigeon leaped up at her approach, fluttered off. She did not run. She did not hurry. She just kept walking. She heard the chant behind her. "Gimme an L—*L*. Gimme an I—*I*." The security guard saw her coming. He held the door like she was entering a fancy restaurant.

When it was over and she was back at the hotel, Lenore found that those few minutes on the sidewalk talking to Bliss stood out in her memory more clearly than anything that had happened inside the clinic. She felt guilty, no surprise in and of itself, but the reasons for her guilt were not the ones she might have expected. She worried that Bliss's mother had gotten mad at her for failing to take advantage of an opportunity to preach the message of their faith. She wondered if Bliss was concerned about the state of Lenore's soul—perhaps she was praying for her even now—or for her own soul, given the fact that she'd let Lenore off the hook without confrontation. What were the heavenly consequences for doing nothing? Lenore had no idea, and she felt guilty about that, too, though she supposed it was equally possible that Bliss had written Lenore off as another heathen damned to hell or that she took a less personal, win-some-lose-some approach to saving the unborn.

The waiting room had smelled of vanilla. Lenore remembered that. The receptionist was burning a scented candle on her desk. A nurse in purple scrubs led Lenore down the hall to a plain white room with a sink and cabinets filled with medical supplies and a gurney covered with paper sheets. A second nurse arrived to ask her a series of questions: *Did she have any allergies? A history of mental illness? Was she sexually active? How many partners?*

This second nurse, Lenore remembered, had a birthmark shaped like Australia on her throat. She was the one who assisted the doctor with the procedure. Lenore couldn't remember what the doctor looked like at all. He was just a voice in her head telling her what he was doing between her legs. *I'm going to insert a speculum, Lenore* and *You'll feel my fingers now* and *Now I'm going to give you a local anesthetic*. She remembered a tremendous and terrible pressure, like her secret was finally too much to contain.

Eventually, somebody must have called her a cab, though she had no memory of the trip back to the hotel or paying the driver or walking through the lobby or riding the elevator up to her room. She dropped onto one of the beds and plummeted into sleep as if falling out of consciousness from a great height. She dreamed that she and Bliss were at Disney World together, but Bliss believed that Space Mountain was sacrilegious for reasons Lenore failed to understand. It was dark out when she woke, pamphlets scattered on the mattress beside her along with a box of menstrual pads someone at the clinic must have given her. There was a care and recovery pamphlet organized as a list of common questions and their answers: *How long before I can resume normal activities? Will I cramp and bleed? What if I still feel pregnant? How do I prevent infection? What sort of complications can occur?* There was also a pamphlet about counseling and a prescription for antibiotics. Lenore balled the pamphlets into a wad and dropped them in the trash.

She slept and listened to music on her headphones and watched pay-per-view movies in her room. With tax, the movies ran almost ten dollars each, and because she hadn't provided a credit card, she had to go down to the front desk to pay in advance each time. She did the math, figured she had enough money left for two movies and one meal per day, usually a grilled chicken salad or soup and bread. She paid cash for her meals as well, which irritated the waiters because they had to return to the restaurant to make change, then haul her change up to her room again. She didn't have enough money to tip what they deserved. She watched *The Fugitive* and *Groundhog Day* and *Mrs. Doubtfire*. She quit *Schindler's List* halfway through. Twice, she watched *Jurassic Park*. She hung the *Do Not Disturb* sign on the doorknob and dozed between movies. She ached. She bled. One night the bleeding was so heavy it soaked through the pad, and she woke to find her thighs and belly smeared, sheets like a crime scene. She was too ashamed to let housekeeping clean the mess, so she simply made the bed and moved into the spare.

She remembered to call home so her mother wouldn't get suspicious.

"I was just thinking about you," her mother said.

"Yeah?"

"Do you remember Emma Gray?"

"Fifth grade? Took forever to lose her baby teeth?"

"If you say so, sweetie. I'm having lunch with her mom. We're on the planning committee for the Friends of Literacy ball."

"Fun," Lenore said.

The next morning, she showered and shaved her legs and gave her teeth a thorough brushing. She dressed in clean blue jeans and a plain black V-necked sweater that she liked. She rode the elevator to the lobby and passed the front desk without acknowledging the clerks and then out through the revolving doors into the bright wave of the day. She couldn't stop blinking in the light. Was it Thursday or Friday? She wasn't sure. On Saturday, she would cab out to the airport with her duffel bag and meet Melissa at the baggage claim like she'd just flown into town. She'd spend one night with the Chens before she and Melissa returned to Briarwood on Sunday morning.

Lenore walked for two blocks before she realized that she was headed in the wrong direction. She repeated the word *obelisk* in her head as she walked back the other way—*obelisk*, *obelisk*.

Already a crowd on the Mall. Joggers, tourists. White-haired veterans in American Legion caps in front of the Air and Space Museum. They, too, were carrying protest signs, and Lenore wondered what these old soldiers could possibly object to in the Air and Space Museum. The signs all bore a woman's name: *Enola Gay*. One of the veterans asked Lenore to sign a petition, but she kept walking up the steps into the gaping hangar of the entry hall. Admission was free, but Lenore had to stand in line to buy a ticket to the planetarium movie—eight more bucks she couldn't afford to spend. She found a seat and waited until the auditorium faded black. Radiant prisms rippled into being. Shimmering clouds of gas. Planets like gaudy baubles spinning through perfect emptiness. Black holes. Solar flares. Bliss was right. The show was dizzying, worth the expense. It felt almost holy. Darkness everywhere and everywhere beautiful light. The narrator had a British accent. "The deeper into space we look," he said, "the further back in time we see."

Question 5

On December 21, 1993, home from boarding school, Lenore Littlefield was dragged to a Christmas party by her mother. There were other young people at the party, a number of them boys, and to her surprise Lenore had fun, sneaking swallows from a bottle of Beefeater swiped from the bar. With whom did she slip away?

A) The son of the hosts, returned from Clemson for the holidays.

B) A boy she'd had a crush on in middle school but hadn't seen in years.

C) The thief who stole the Beefeater in the first place.

D) None of the above.

XVIII

Despite everything, the bell rang on Monday morning at its appointed hour, some poor freshman at the end of the rope, and by the hundred, the girls shuffled off to class, still half-asleep, still half-lost in their dreams, all of them so young, their lives more future than past. They didn't know anything. They would make so many mistakes. Lenore shouldered her backpack. Art History and Latin and Algebra II and American History and Chemistry and American Lit, in that order.

At five o'clock she reported to the auditorium, where she dissolved and was reconstituted as someone else. There was no pretense in her portrayal of Jenny March. She was released from herself. She ran her lines. She hit her marks. She saw herself rising from the bed. Her lips were moving. The words came to her unbidden, even after a week without rehearsal. She heard Coach Fink's whistle as if from a distance, and there passed a stretch when Lenore felt in between things, herself and not herself, aware but not aware of Coach Fink striding toward center stage.

"Everybody huddle up," Coach Fink said.

The girls arranged themselves on the beds or on the floor between them like a slumber party. Coach Fink was brimming. She swung her arms and pressed up and down on her toes while she waited for them to settle. Then she began to speak, and it took a minute for Lenore to register what her coach was saying, partly because she was still hovering in that disembodied place and partly because the words themselves were so unlikely. Coach Fink told the girls how Mr. Bishop had tracked down Eugenia Marsh's address and how they drove to Rockbridge County and how they found Eugenia Marsh cleaning her gutters. She repeated what she claimed was Eugenia Marsh's advice about *The Phantom of Thornton Hall*, something about keeping the mystery behind you. "I'm not gonna bullshit you, ladies," Coach Fink said. She made it clear that Eugenia Marsh had in no way promised to come for opening night. The very idea, however, that Coach Fink had actually met Eugenia Marsh, had shaken her hand and seen the inside of her house and returned bearing advice from her own lips, the very possibility that Eugenia Marsh might witness their performance of her play in person, sent a ripple through the cast, and when Coach Fink was finished, Juliet Demarinis led them all in a long round of applause.

And still the bell clanged them on toward the dining hall after rehearsal like nothing had changed. The same placid stars, the same mellow darkness hovering over campus and nestling in the trees. The dining hall blazed with light and chatter, humidity rising from the buffet, the smell like meat boiled in bleach. At last, the bedtime rituals. Girls lined up at the sinks to brush their teeth and scrub their faces. Numerous antiacne agents were brought to bear. The row of their reflections might have belonged to any of the girls who'd ever lived in Thornton Hall. In an old T-shirt and flannel boxers, Lenore shuffled back to her room, where Melissa was putting the finishing touches on a coat of toenail polish.

She asked some question, and Lenore said something in reply, and they went on like that for what must have been half an hour. Then the lights were out, and Lenore was on her side, facing the wall, with the blanket drawn over her shoulder. Somehow she'd left her Walkman in DC, and without the music she couldn't make her mind go quiet. Lines from the play flicked through her head all out of order—*I have never been a wary girl* and *I think we dream so we can forget* and *A shadow is only interrupted light*—and she had the curious sense that the wall inches from her nose was just a scrim. She could reach out her fingers and push right through it, not into the next room but to some hazy other side, where Jenny March might take her hand, and she would pass through time and space, from this life into a dream, neither one stranger than the other. Dreaming, then, but not quite dreaming, lines from the play still repeating like faraway voices in her thoughts, vaguely aware of the too warm pillow beneath her ear and of the fact that her feet had escaped her blankets and of the phone ringing down the hall, a reverberation that seemed at first to be coming from inside her, vibrating through her, but that gradually resolved into what it was and returned her to herself.

She flopped onto her back and waited for someone to answer. Husna most likely. Her room was nearest to the phone closet. But it kept on ringing and ringing until it stopped,

Lenore acutely conscious of the quiet in the absence of the sound. She looked at Melissa, lips parted, hair fanned around her face. Definitely zonked. Lenore alone in her wakefulness. She flipped her pillow to the cool side. She could remember drifting off to sleep when she was a girl, before the divorce, her parents settling in for a drink in the living room, their tired, tipsy voices murmuring her into dreams.

The phone began to ring again.

At that hour the sound meant family emergency or desperate boy, so Lenore huffed and tossed aside her blankets and hustled out the door, but the phone stopped ringing the instant she arrived.

Lenore hit the light switch and eyed the receiver for a few seconds as if daring it to ring again, and then she shut the door behind her and sat on the floor with her arms around her knees. It was almost cozy in there, all those phone numbers and all that graffiti on the walls somehow reassuring, a reminder that lives existed beyond her own—Domino's Pizza delivery and *Save Us Kurt Cobain* and J. Crew customer service and *My Mother Is a Dick* and dorm extensions at the Woodmont School and *Dicks Are People Too* and a pretty decent ballpoint sketch of a cat smoking a joint and a number that would tell you the time in Mobile, Alabama. Lenore pushed to her feet and lifted the receiver. Dialed information.

"I need a listing in Charleston, last name Rawlings."

Faint ticking on the operator's end.

"I've got a bunch of Rawlings in Charleston."

"Do any of them show a children's line?"

"Matter of fact, yes," the operator said. "Hold for your listing," and her voice was replaced by a mechanical recitation spooling off the digits one by one as if each bore no relation to the others. There was a nub of pencil on the floor, and Lenore used it to jot the number on the wall, unremarkable among the others. Nate Rawlings. She had no plans to call him. She didn't know if she wanted to call him. Or what she would say to him if she did. She wasn't even sure this was his number. That night had been a mistake, true, but nothing terrible, she thought, nothing unforgivable—right?—and maybe she was fooling herself, but there was sweetness in the memory, shame and regret barreling down only after the fact. Nate had thanked her when they finished, real gratitude in his voice and something else as well, something like awe.

When she hung up, the phone rang in her hand, and Lenore snatched her fingers away like she'd been shocked. It did not ring a second time. She lifted the receiver, listened. Just a dial tone. The bulb in the phone closet flickered out. Lenore tried the switch, but it was dead. She peeked out of the phone closet—abandoned couches, flyers on the bulletin board, television blank as slate. The only light seeped down the stairs from a fixture on the landing, and as Lenore moved out of the phone closet it faltered, blinking off and on before building in intensity like the laziest power surge in the world. The air in her mouth tasted cold. She hugged herself and rubbed her arms. And that light—it kept on getting brighter and slowly brighter, the landing illuminated as if beneath a spotlight on a stage. Any second now, she thought, and a figure would appear, bending around the landing, edging closer. "Who's there?" she said. The light, the cold. The deserted common room. Then she saw it, the shape of it, barely visible, no more substance than light itself, the vaguest outline of a woman made of nothing, made of air, made of light, the shape of her wavering like flame. "Who's there?" Lenore said again, and the shape was gone, the light extinguished, nothing but darkness all around.

Behind her, after a moment, the ringing of the phone.

Slowly, warily, with her heart pounding and her arms held out before her like a blind man, Lenore followed the sound, feeling for the door frame of the phone closet and running her hand along the wall until she found the phone itself, jumping shrilly in its cradle as it rang. The phone rang again beneath her hand, and this time she brought it to her ear.

"Hello?"

Down the line a rushing like the inside of a seashell, and behind that, faintly, Lenore heard a voice say, "Don't," a woman's voice, she thought, though it was impossible to be sure, the voice quavering and broken as if sifted through the spinning blades of a fan.

"Don't what?" Lenore said.

"Don't call him."

The voice clearer now and closer, that seashell rush fading away with Lenore's fear. "Elizabeth?" she said.

"You can never tell him what you did."

"This is crazy," Lenore said. "I was in bed and I was almost asleep. I must still be in bed. I dreamed the phone was ringing."

The light in the phone closet stuttered back to life, and suddenly Lenore was looking at the knuckles of her free hand, her fingers splayed against the wall beside the phone, the word *please* creeping out from under her palm. The rushing sound washed in and then diminished, like a wave against the beach. She had the palpable sense that someone was waiting for her to speak.

"He was so nice," she said.

"I know."

"He had these eyes."

"I know."

"I wish none of this had happened."

"But it did," Elizabeth said.

Lenore let her head tip forward until her brow was resting on her knuckles. This close, the graffiti squiggled and swam.

"Why?" she said, a question that might have applied to many things, but she figured Elizabeth's ghost would catch her meaning.

"You remind me of a girl I used to know."

XIX

Coach Fink marched down the hill after rehearsal, twirling her whistle around her hand, pinching the string in place with her thumb and looping the whistle clockwise through the air, then swiftly counterclockwise, the string tightening in such a way that each rotation brought the whistle to rest with a satisfying smack against her palm. Just enough light left in the sky to sketch the outlines of the trees. As she approached the doors to Ransom Library, it occurred to her that she'd been coaching at Briarwood for thirteen years but hadn't crossed the threshold in all that time. To tell the truth, she hadn't spent much time in the library in her student days. It hadn't changed—the vaulted ceilings, the arched windows, the chandeliers, smart girls hunched over their homework at the study tables. Apprehension fizzed in Coach Fink like she was sixteen again and had a paper due in the morning about some novel she hadn't read.

"Can I help you?"

A librarian in cat's-eye glasses presided over everything from a stool behind the circulation desk.

"I'm looking for a PBS production of *The Phantom of Thornton Hall*."

The librarian removed her glasses. For a second her features went still, as if she were posing for a photograph. Then she wrinkled her eyebrows and said, "You don't remember me, do you? I was a year behind you in school. Constance Booth? Connie? I was the assistant stage manager when you played Maria in *West Side Story*."

Coach Fink studied her face, searching for anything familiar in her eyes, her mouth. She could recall how Wilson Barber's voice had cracked on the high notes of "Tonight" and how Virginia Cross, as Anita, had mixed up the lyrics in "A Boy Like That," singing, "Forget that boy and find your mother," instead of "Forget that boy and find another." She could remember the bone-deep quality of her stage fright, so pervasive it had a taste—like cold coffee. She could remember the scorched smell of the footlights and the shapes of people in the crowd. But she could not remember Connie Booth.

Her silence provided ample confirmation.

"My hair was different then," said Connie Booth, and she turned on her ballet flats and disappeared through the door behind her desk. Reappeared half a minute later. "That video is checked out."

"Does Bishop have it still?"

"Library policy prohibits me from releasing that information."

All these women on their stools with their paltry secrets. Coach Fink resisted the urge to blow her whistle just to make a little noise.

* * *

Her best bet, Coach Fink thought, was to go straight to the source. The problem was she hadn't spoken to Bishop since Rockbridge County. This was not unusual. Before their road trip, whole weeks would often pass without seeing or thinking of Bishop until she bumped into him on the quad or noticed him stepping down from the bleachers after a basketball game. Her recurring dream had tapered off, which might have been a relief if Bishop hadn't seeped into her unconscious to take its place. These new dreams weren't erotic in the least—the two of them paddling a canoe or shooting hoops or, for some reason, building a tree house—but she woke dry-mouthed and aroused. The last thing Coach Fink needed was that sort of distraction, not with opening night so close. She trooped back up the hill beneath the oaks toward Bishop's duplex, a new and different sort of apprehension bubbling in her. She told herself that all she wanted was to see if Bishop still had the PBS version of *The Phantom of Thornton Hall*. And there he was, sitting on the stoop outside his duplex like she'd conjured him up with repressed desire.

Beside him, to Coach Fink's surprise, was Lenore Littlefield, Bishop's dog sprawled between them with his head in Littlefield's lap, all three of them so absorbed that they'd failed to notice her approach. Faculty cars were parked along the curb, and without thinking Coach Fink took two steps to her right and ducked behind a station wagon, owned, she thought, by Lionel Higgins. Before her eyes a bumper sticker: *I Brake for Michelangelo*.

"What was she like?" Littlefield was saying.

"What was who like?"

"Eugenia Marsh. You met her, right? Everybody's curious."

"She was nice, I guess. We didn't stay long."

"Did she seem happy?"

"Lenore," Bishop said.

"Somebody asked me not too long ago if I thought happiness was even possible or if we spend so much time pretending that we've forgotten what real happiness feels like."

Eavesdropping was not Coach Fink's style. She was much more likely to barge into a situation whatever it might be. She couldn't have explained the impulse that had caused her to dart behind the car, but now she wasn't sure how to extract herself. She wasn't sure she wanted to extract herself. She was bothered by the idea of Bishop fraternizing after hours with a student, and if something was going on with her lead actress, something that might affect the play, Coach Fink wanted to know about it, but mostly she couldn't help wondering if Bishop might say her name. She was part of this story, too. She had met Eugenia Marsh. Rummaged her cabinets for a mixing bowl. She had waited with Bishop in her truck, the night crazy with stars.

"It must be strange. For you. Playing Jenny." He was speaking so slowly that Coach Fink had the sense he was choosing his words with care. "It must be. Hard."

"I like it," Littlefield said. "It's a relief."

They were quiet for a moment. Coach Fink shifted on her haunches.

"You remember the last scene?" Littlefield went on. "When Jenny walks over to the window and she stands there staring out at the dark, and the play just ends with her still standing there. You can hardly believe it's over. You have no idea what happens next."

"I remember," Bishop said.

"I used to think it was a cop-out, but I don't think so anymore."

"Lenore," he said again.

"It was just an abortion," Littlefield said, and Coach Fink gripped the bumper of the station wagon like she intended to yank it off with her bare hands. She didn't understand everything she was hearing, but the intimacy between them felt illicit, and worst-case scenarios scurried through her mind, and she knew that, whatever she was hearing, it was terrible somehow. She understood that she would never forget this night, not a single detail, not Connie Booth or the stupid bumper sticker or the ache in Bishop's voice when he spoke Littlefield's name, and this understanding sickened her. They were still talking, but she couldn't make out their words over the pulse whomping in her head. She had no idea how much time had passed before she realized that nobody was saying anything anymore. She peeked around the bumper, but they were gone.

Then she could feel herself moving closer to Bishop's door, almost floating, the door drifting nearer until she was so close she could see brushstrokes in the paint. Part of her already regretted what she did not know she was about to do. She knocked, and Bishop opened the door, and at the sight of him, before he'd said a word, before she'd had time to register the pleasantly surprised look on his face, she grabbed his shoulders for leverage and brought her knee up into his balls, dropping him like he'd been shot. He clutched himself with both hands, half in the house, half on the stoop. The sound he made put her in mind of a cold engine failing to start. Pickett trotted over to sniff Bishop's ear, then the back of Coach Fink's hand. The video was right there on top of his TV. She stepped over Bishop and crossed the room. "I'm taking this," she said. Bishop was struggling to his feet, leaning heavily on the jamb, and she kicked him from behind on her way out, her foot wedging itself neatly into his groin, the breath whooshing out of him, his body curling like a question mark on the floor.

What she should have done was go directly to Briarwood Manor, inform Headmistress Mackey of her suspicions, let somebody more qualified take it from there, but momentum carried her down the hill toward Thornton Hall, the videotape clutched like a discus in her right hand.

She barged through the double doors and past the students watching TV in the common room, their heads swiveling as she passed, and then up the stairs and down the hall to the room she'd visited once before. There was Demarinis, belly-down in bed, textbook open, but Littlefield's mattress had been stripped, the walls bare on her side of the room, and Coach Fink had the sense that time was roaring past while she stood still. She heard a buzz from somewhere, the sound growing louder until it became a rattle, like a beetle on its back. A clock on the dresser, the minute flipping into place. She pointed at the empty bed.

"Where's Littlefield?"

"She moved," Demarinis said. "After Poppy left, she moved in with Melissa Chen. First floor."

Back down the stairs then and through the common room and along the first-floor hall, shouldering doors open as she went, but all she met were the blankly astonished faces of girls who were not Littlefield.

Behind the seventh door she startled a pretty Asian girl folding laundry.

"Excuse you," the girl said, bringing a towel up to her chest like she was naked, though Coach Fink could plainly see that she was dressed.

"Does Littlefield live here?"

"She's on the phone," the girl said, and Coach Fink slammed the door on her way out.

Past the bathroom, girls with toothpaste at the corners of their mouths poking their heads out to track her progress, and past the bulletin board, flyers promoting *The Phantom of Thornton Hall* rustling in her wake, all of this imprinting in her memory, overlaying existing memories of a thousand meaningless passages down this hall. In the bright light of the common room it began to dawn on Coach Fink that she was causing a commotion. She forced herself to slow down. Breathe. She rapped three times on the door of the phone closet.

Through the little window she could see surprise pass like a shadow over Littlefield's face but no guilt or fear or sorrow, no reflection of what she had overheard, nothing like the wash of emotion still surging in Coach Fink. Littlefield held up a finger for her to wait, then mouthed a few words into the phone, listened for a second, hung up. She stepped into the common room, looking confused.

"That was my mom," she said. "She's coming to the play."

Coach Fink could sense the girls on the couches pricking their ears, feel their eyes on her back, could hear dribbles of TV laughter. Littlefield swiped her hair behind her ear.

Just then, Coach Fink remembered what she was holding in her hand.

"You want to watch a video?" she said.

Coach Fink's office was tucked away in a back corner of the locker room, the locker room tucked away in a back corner of the gym. The majority of the space, not much to begin with, was taken up by a chain-link cage, in which could be found a decades-long accretion of athletic equipment: mesh bags bulging with basketballs, chipped and battered field hockey sticks, orange plastic cones, old jerseys and shorts, cardboard boxes of athletic wrap and tape, stopwatches, whistles, dozens of pairs of cleats and high-tops her girls had left behind, frayed towels in laundry bags, liniments in crusty tubes, milk crates containing trophies that Coach Fink had neither the space nor the inclination to display, their proud miniature heads and triumphant miniature arms poking into sight above the rims. The accumulated contents of the equipment cage wafted faintly of menthol and wet rags. Coach Fink never bothered to take inventory—if she needed something, it was always in there—but she was confident that a significant portion of the cage's contents had been around since Delores Udall's day.

An ancient metal desk and swivel chair, also formerly Delores Udall's, were shoved against the wall, and there was a metal folding chair for guests. Coach Fink had spent countless afternoons in that chair as a student, picking Coach Udall's brain about technique, but she didn't think Littlefield had ever set foot in the office until tonight, except perhaps to notify Coach Fink that she'd be late to practice for one reason or another, and it was strange to see her in that chair, her eyes focused on the TV, on a trolley in the corner, *The Phantom of Thornton Hall* flickering on the screen.

There was something strange as well about watching these familiar actresses, Sissy Spacek and the one whose name escaped Coach Fink, their familiar voices speaking those familiar lines on the heels of what Coach Fink had seen and heard this night but still failed to understand, the set on-screen nearly identical to the set onstage in Garvey Auditorium.

It was this strangeness, all these layers of strangeness, that made it possible, finally, for Coach Fink to speak.

"I heard you talking to Mr. Bishop."

Littlefield tensed—Coach Fink could see it in her shoulders, her neck—but did not look away from the TV.

"Did Mr. Bishop," Coach Fink said, and then she stopped. "Did he—did he do something? Something he shouldn't have? With you?"

"No. Nothing like that."

"Are you sure? Because if he did—"

"You've definitely got the wrong idea."

"I'm afraid I'm gonna need an explanation," Coach Fink said.

The office was dark but for the TV and quiet but for its sound, and Littlefield did not say anything for what seemed to Coach Fink like a very long time, just the dialogue from the play in the air between them, Coach Fink looking at Littlefield, Littlefield intent on *The Phantom of Thornton Hall*. When she did begin to speak, the details weren't as awful as Coach Fink had feared, though her disgust with Bishop was undiminished. A part of her wished she hadn't reacted so violently before she was in possession of the facts, but that part of her was easily convinced to pipe down by the part of her that had had sex with Bishop in a motel room in Rockbridge County while he knew—*he knew*—that Littlefield was pregnant. That part of her wanted to kick him in the balls again. On-screen, Jenny stood and walked over to the window, and Coach Fink thumbed pause on the remote, freezing Sissy Spacek in her white nightgown.

"I hate every bit of this," she said.

That dense strangeness washed over her again, here in her office with a recently pregnant teenage boarding-school student watching Sissy Spacek's portrayal of a fictionally pregnant teenage boarding-school student in a play written by a woman who had been a student at the very school where Coach Fink herself had been a student not so long ago.

There remained a number of details to hash out, decisions to be made, but all that could wait a few more minutes. For now, Coach Fink pressed rewind on the remote, and they watched Sissy Spacek walking backward away from the window and sitting backward on her bed, where she talked backward to Eleanor Bowman's ghost, her mouth swallowing up the words she'd already said, before Coach Fink pressed play, and the images rolled forward again on-screen. Bishop had been right about one thing. Sissy Spacek was amazing. No matter what her Jenny was talking about, no matter how trivial the subject, isolation and despair were always just beneath the surface. She exuded them somehow. In her tone, her body language. Those feelings crept over you like a chill.

XX

The study of history had taught Bishop to expect the worst, so he was not surprised when Valerie summoned him to Headmistress Mackey's office in the morning. Valerie did not stand when he arrived, nor did she greet him with her customary cheerfulness. She simply buzzed Headmistress Mackey on the intercom and said, "He's here," and Bishop was certain that Coach Fink had told them everything.

He had used the hours after Coach Fink's ambush to erase himself with booze, feet up on the couch, a bag of frozen peas over his genitals. She must have overheard, misunderstood. Or maybe she'd understood perfectly. He had wanted to chase after her, bang on her door. He had wanted to explain but he couldn't imagine the words. Eventually he passed out, with a whiskey propped in his lap, the bag of frozen peas keeping it cold. By the time he woke up, the drink had spilled, the peas had melted, and the phone was bleating in the kitchen, Valerie calling bright and early to bid him to his reckoning.

Headmistress Mackey was waiting in the swivel chair behind her desk, back to Bishop, facing the window. "Sit," she said, and Bishop did.

The office was large enough to accommodate a sofa and a coffee table and matching armchairs, built-in bookshelves along one wall, but in Bishop's experience, Headmistress Mackey only ever conducted business from behind her desk. Two more chairs—uncomfortable, wooden, spindle-backed—were positioned on the desk's other side, and it was in one of these that he waited, hangover roiling in his hands, his stomach, his eyes, his joints, his scalp. Only her head was visible, her hair almost sculptural from this angle. Finally, Headmistress Mackey swiveled to face him, tossing a section of the *Washington Post* onto her desk.

"Have you seen this morning's editorial page?"

"Not yet," he said. "No, ma'am."

"I'll tell you something, Mr. Bishop. I weary of speculation regarding traffic problems and insufficient infrastructure and low-wage service-sector jobs. I'm certain that the good people who need those Disney jobs would offer a markedly different take."

"I'm sure you're right."

"I have half a mind to cancel our subscription."

She settled back in her chair with an index finger pressed against her lips. He had the idea that she was attempting to read his thoughts, tendrils of her psyche probing his subconscious.

"It has come to my attention," she began, but Bishop cut her off before he had a chance to change his mind.

"I'll quit," he said. "I'll just quit."

He'd been considering this possibility ever since he hung up with Valerie Beech. Before that even—he had sensed the notion rising, half formed, from the depths of his inebriation, but it hadn't quite reached the surface. He'd made a mistake, and he deserved to suffer for it, and no sense delaying the inevitable. But Headmistress Mackey made an exasperated face, fanning his resignation away like a stink.

"Under other circumstances," she said, "I might find your eagerness to throw yourself on your sword commendable, but today it strikes me as a waste of resources and entirely unnecessary and more dramatic than I would have expected from you. It's true that I was—how shall I put it?—justifiably perturbed that you and Coach Fink sought out Eugenia Marsh. I'd hoped our previous conversation would leave a more permanent impression. I'll admit I was surprised when Valerie told me what she'd heard. I was also a tad impressed. I wouldn't have believed you had it in you."

Bishop opened his mouth. Closed it. His teeth made a clacking sound inside his head, and behind the sound of his teeth, a fog came wisping into his mind. He could almost see it swirling around in there, layering itself between what he heard and his ability to comprehend.

"Have you talked to Coach Fink?" he said.

Headmistress Mackey twitched the corners of her mouth into a grin. "I've known Patricia Fink for a long time, Mr. Bishop. Her record in the gym and on the field is unimpeachable, but perspicacity is not high among her strengths. Her role in all this is easily chalked up to foolishness. Your role, however, smacks of rebellion."

"You brought me here to talk about Eugenia Marsh?" he said.

"Nothing that happens at this school escapes my attention, Mr. Bishop."

He imagined the news traveling across campus like water in a bucket brigade. Coach Fink had told the cast, and one of the cast members had told her roommate, and her roommate had told a teacher, and that teacher told Valerie Beech, who told Headmistress Mackey, who required a word with Bishop to douse the blaze.

"I brought you here," she went on, "to inform you that I have decided to second your invitation. Make it official. We'll celebrate opening night in her honor. We can't rename the auditorium of course, but I see no reason that we can't dedicate the stage. The Eugenia Marsh Stage in the Beatrix Garvey Memorial Auditorium." She tipped her head from side to side, considering. "Inelegant, but it will do. We'll need permission from the Garvey family and approval from the board, but those things can be arranged. If Ms. Marsh is anything like the unruly girl she was at Briarwood or the batty recluse portrayed by the media, I'm confident that institutional endorsement and public ceremony should be just the combination to ensure she stays away."

Now she leaned back in her chair, her triumph over him revealed. She let her wrists droop from the armrests. Bishop worried he might be sick. Headmistress Mackey crossed her legs, smoothed her skirt.

"I refuse to accept your resignation," she said, "because I'm putting you in charge of the opening-night festivities. I should think that's punishment enough. I require someone to liaise with the caterer and the florist. The program must be proofed and printed. Valerie has gotten the ball rolling, but she can't do all the work herself."

"I thought—" Bishop said, but the rest of the sentence was lost in the fog.

Headmistress Mackcy finished on his behalf. "You thought Ms. Marsh might stir up enough trouble that I would reconsider our affiliation with Disney. That sound about right, Mr. Bishop? Eugenia Marsh has made her opposition to Disney's America public. She makes it *newsworthy*." This last word she dragged out in a disgusted way.

Nausea rushed over him like a wave and then receded, leaving Bishop breathless with self-loathing.

"Let us understand each other, Mr. Bishop. Disney's check is in the bank. We've received a number of additional pledges from prominent alumnae, and I have no intention of disappointing them. I intend to break ground on the computer lab next fall whether Eugenia Marsh attends the play or not. Let her come, let her stir up trouble. She'll only be making a monkey of herself. Your job is to see to it that Briarwood welcomes her with a celebration befitting the prodigal's return."

She stood and rapped her knuckles on the desk, and Bishop lurched to his feet. He paused at the door, Valerie's typewriter ticking in the anteroom. In a few more seconds, he would rejoin the steady stream of his life. Teach his classes, walk his dog. The fog churned in his mind like some huge thing was moving through it. Then he opened the door and hurried past Valerie's desk and down the stairs and ducked into the men's room on the first floor, where he vomited into the toilet. There was only one. Facilities for men were scarce at an all-girls' school. When he was finished, he rinsed his mouth and washed his hands and crossed the quad to Everett Hall.

His classes had moved on to the 1960s, and Bishop decided to run an episode of a civil rights documentary called *Eyes on the Prize*. Technically, *Eyes on the Prize* wasn't scheduled until Friday, but he was too wrecked to manage a discussion. For the rest of the morning, he watched the old footage and listened to the scholars and eyewitnesses, the classroom muggy, his students lolling in their desks. Finally, the fourth-period bell rang, releasing everyone to lunch, and Bishop slumped in his chair, rubbed his eyes. His hangover had consolidated in his face. When he looked again, Lenore was the only other person in the room.

"I talked to Coach Fink," she said.

Bishop had figured as much. If Coach Fink hadn't told Headmistress Mackey, she must have gone straight to Lenore.

"How'd you get her to keep your secret?"

Lenore shrugged. "It's just until after the play. Then I have to report to Mrs. Silver or Coach Fink will dime me out."

He waited to see if more information might be forthcoming, but she just stood there beside his desk watching him, with her thumbs hooked under the straps of her backpack, as if waiting for him to speak as well.

"I'm sorry, Lenore," he said.

On his desk, between his stapler and a coffee cup filled with ballpoint pens, sat a globe the size of an apple, a thank-you gift from a former student, though at the moment he couldn't recall which one, a paperweight printed with an antique version of the world, misshapen and misnamed continents, sea monsters emerging from the deep, and Bishop picked it up and rolled it palm to palm.

"What for? You didn't do anything."

"That's what for," Bishop said.

Lenore held her hand out, and it took Bishop a second to realize that she was asking for the globe. He passed it over. Lenore frowned as if that version of the world gave her a headache.

"I know how you can make it up to me," she said.

At the end of the day, he loaded Pickett in the car, and they drove out to the Disney site. They walked deep into the woods, medallions of light spilling through the branches. Pickett flashed like a figment among the trees. Bishop had wanted to get away from campus, clear his head, consider Lenore's proposal in peace. He thought of Lenore in the snow on the day she told him she was pregnant. Of Lenore on his stoop after Poppy was suspended. Of Lenore alone in some wretched clinic.

Now she wanted them, Bishop and Coach Fink, to drive her to Rockbridge County. She required a meeting with Eugenia Marsh. She wouldn't say why exactly, though apparently Coach Fink had already agreed. They would leave early Saturday morning and return to Briarwood before curfew. He'd told Lenore he'd think about it, but no amount of thinking made her proposal sound like a good idea. It wasn't so much the idea of dropping in on Eugenia Marsh again that made him hesitant. And it wasn't fear of how Headmistress Mackey might react if she caught wind of their excursion. His job seemed the least he could risk for Lenore. What made him hesitant was the idea of spending a day in close quarters with Coach Fink. It didn't matter that she knew the truth. He remained the agent of her unhappiness. Still, he didn't see how he could refuse.

Back on campus, night wisping down over the grounds, he pocketed Pickett's tennis ball and patted his hip for the dog to follow and positioned himself in the dell between Faculty Row and Briarwood Manor. Rehearsal would be wrapping up soon, and he intended to intercept Coach Fink on her way home. A chance meeting beneath the oaks. He was just tossing a ball with his dog, and she was just on her way home from rehearsal. He would confirm her agreement and that was all. He must have chucked the ball fifty times before Pickett tired of retrieving and hunkered down under a tree with his tongue hanging out and Bishop sat beside him on a root.

While they waited, lights flickered on in the windows of Briarwood Manor, Headmistress Mackey in there somewhere, the silver Jaguar in the driveway indicating that her husband was in town. It was a beautiful old Palladian-style house, the brick a worn, rusty brown, impressive without being ostentatious. Sometimes Bishop could stand under the oaks, most of them older than the house itself, and imagine this place before the school, the house alone atop the hill, looking down the slope of the lawn, past a cluster of long-gone outbuildings, a smokehouse and slave cottages leveled to make way for the quad, and on down to the stable at the bottom of the hill, original to the estate, could imagine the horses in the paddock as the same horses that had been here more than a hundred years ago. Headmistress Mackey hosted receptions for faculty and students and their parents in

Briarwood Manor, and there was no denying the presence of history in that place. Union soldiers had died in those rooms when the house served as a hospital after Second Manassas. And young girls had studied there in the early days of the school. And generations of Brunson children had been born under that roof before Charlotte's sons were killed in the Civil War and she allowed the school to be created. Bishop could stand beneath the trees sometimes and feel the past swirling around him like a current. But this was not one of those times.

There—a cluster of girls milled out of the auditorium, headed for the dining hall. A minute later Coach Fink appeared under the exterior lights with Lenore. She rested her hands on Lenore's shoulders. Lenore bobbed her head at whatever Coach Fink was saying. It was like watching TV with the volume muted. Finally, Lenore trailed off after her cast mates and Coach Fink trudged up the hill, swinging her arms. Pickett trotted down to meet her, gave her knees a sniff. Coach Fink ignored the dog and glared at Bishop, her body leaning slightly against the grade.

"I'm taking Littlefield to Rockbridge County."

"I know," Bishop said. "I'll drive."

XXI

They talked every night, and every night it was the same, the phone ringing in the dark and that seashell rushing and then her voice, Elizabeth's voice, wavering down the line. They talked about clothes. They talked about roommates. They talked about boys. Somehow they were never interrupted. There was nothing profound in these conversations. They did not discuss the possibility of true love or the nature of death or the inevitability of sorrow. Elizabeth shared no insight regarding the mysteries of the beyond. They talked about teachers and Drama Club. They talked about Poppy. They talked about Eugenia Marsh, not as she was now but as she had been, rambunctious and defiant and baffled by her life.

"She told me once that she wished she was a nun," Elizabeth said.

"Was she religious?"

"She liked their clothes."

"You're kidding."

"She said they looked romantic, all covered up, everything but their hands and faces."

"I'm nervous," Lenore said.

"Don't be. She'll be glad you found her."

They never said good-bye, at least not that Lenore was able to recall, and she never could remember hanging up the phone. One minute she was talking to Elizabeth, the next she was waking up right where she started, light seeping in under the blinds. And so it was on Saturday morning, Lenore blinking suddenly awake, the clock on her nightstand glowing, 6:54 a.m. Melissa was still asleep, her hands folded neatly on her chest. Lenore pulled a sweatshirt over her head, stepped quickly into her jeans, and carried her shoes into the hall. A sink running upstairs, some early riser brushing her teeth. Lenore crept out the back door, careful to shut it quietly behind her, and sat on the curb beside the dumpsters to wait, the exact same spot she'd waited with Poppy in her last few minutes at Briarwood.

She hadn't spoken with Poppy since Union Station. They'd tried to phone, Lenore and Melissa both, but Poppy's mother always answered, and she was still screening Poppy's calls. One time Lenore called in the morning, hoping to sneak past the defenses by varying her routine, and Poppy's mother let it slip that her daughter was at work, though she didn't say where, and Lenore had been too surprised by the idea to ask. She tried to picture Poppy with a job—manning the hostess stand at Ruby Tuesday? Folding blouses at the Gap?

She heard Mr. Bishop's car ticking around the corner before it appeared, Coach Fink riding shotgun, Pickett hanging his head out of a window in the back seat.

"So what's the plan?" Coach Fink said.

Lenore buckled in and rubbed Pickett's ears while he beat his tail and nudged his head against her chest.

"Eugenia Marsh," she said. "That's the plan."

"You sure this is a good idea?" Mr. Bishop said.

Lenore said, "Pretty sure," and this was more or less the truth. She was having nightly conversations with a dead girl. That was impossible. Far more reasonable to believe that Eugenia Marsh would be present and available simply because Lenore needed her to be, that she would have answers to the questions Lenore didn't know how to ask. Still, she cupped Pickett's head in both hands and let him lick her face to avoid meeting any human eyes.

"No matter what," Coach Fink said, "we're back by curfew."

Pickett settled down once they reached the highway. Mr. Bishop and Coach Fink were mostly quiet. They had, it seemed, decided to handle her with care. There was nothing much to do except watch the world scroll by outside the windows, and there was nothing much to see beyond the crappy little towns with their tire shops, their muffler emporiums. The occasional burst of wildflowers in the median. Lenore was reminded of her family's trip to Disney World, six long hours between Charleston and Orlando, her mother in the passenger seat working hard to distract Lenore from her boredom, her parents' marriage already beyond repair, the trip a last gasp, the place itself a false promise, a fantasy of joy. Lenore looked at the back of Mr. Bishop's head and wondered how it was possible that, even so young, she had failed to notice her parents' unhappiness. But they hadn't seemed unhappy standing in the lines, riding the rides, watching the fireworks. They hadn't seemed unhappy eating corn dogs and buying Mickey Mouse ears. And maybe they hadn't been, she thought. Not for those few days. Maybe the trip had been a respite from whatever ailed their marriage, and maybe that wasn't so bad. Maybe it was possible to pretend your way back to happiness or, at least, for a little while, to forget that you're pretending. That's what she'd tell Poppy next time they spoke.

She leaned forward in her seat. "Coach Fink," she said, her voice too loud in the quiet car, "have you ever been to Disney World?"

Coach Fink wiped a hand over the dashboard, then brushed it off on the leg of her jeans, visibly displeased by the volume of dust she had picked up.

"I've been to Disney World," she said.

Mr. Bishop shot a surprised glance in Coach Fink's direction.

Lenore said, "Did you have fun?"

Coach Fink shrugged. "I was a junior in college. I got selected for a national all-star basketball team, and the prize was a trip to Disney World. Did I have fun? I guess. We got to ride in the parade one night."

"Mr. Bishop hates Disney World."

"I never said that."

Was he blushing all of a sudden? Lenore couldn't be sure, but it looked like the backs of his ears had flooded pink.

"You hate Disney's America," she said.

"*Hate* is the wrong word. I'm not against families having a good time, but they intend to build that park right in the middle one of the most history-rich places in the country, and the way Disney operates is so purely commercial, it's downright mercenary—the movies, the action figures, the theme parks. They don't care if they get it right. They only care about what the customer wants to hear. I don't like the idea of generations of little kids weaned on Disney's version of the past."

"What difference does it make?" Coach Fink said.

Mr. Bishop gripped the wheel with both hands.

"If individual experience molds us into who we are as human beings, then surely community experience—national experience—defines us too. As a group, you know, a tribe. We take pride in the same triumphs, share disappointment in our failures. Our history is what makes us into a country in the first place. The way we perceive ourselves. The reason we feel patriotic when we hear the 'Star-Spangled Banner.' No doubt all history is subjective, but it follows that if we have a false impression of that history, then we have a false impression of who we are."

They had merged onto I-64 by then, traffic streaming along the interstate. Coach Fink cranked her window down halfway, as if to clear the air of Mr. Bishop's words, then rolled it back up and turned in her seat to face Lenore.

"Is this what he's like in class?" she said.

Mr. Bishop's Subaru started acting up just after the exit. He said it felt like the wheel was jerking in his hands. Coach Fink didn't comment at first, but Lenore could see her jaw clenching in profile. They'd driven a few miles from the interstate when Lenore heard a clunking noise, loud, like the engine had suddenly flopped onto its back, and then the motor shuddered quiet. They coasted to a stop on the shoulder, and Coach Fink said, "I told you we should have taken my truck."

"There's not enough room in your truck," Mr. Bishop said.

"There's room enough without the damn dog."

"Right," Mr. Bishop said, opening his door and stepping out. "Three of us jammed onto a bench seat. That sounds great."

"At least my truck would still be running," Coach Fink said.

She got out, too, and stood in the weeds, and they continued their bickering over the roof of the car.

"That little country store's not far from here," Mr. Bishop said. "They'll have a phone. We'll just have to walk."

"Not there. No way. I nearly smacked that woman last time."

"It's too far to backtrack. It'll take too long."

"I'd rather get hit with a shovel than set foot in that crazy woman's store."

"Then why don't you wait with the car?" Mr. Bishop said.

"Maybe I will."

"Maybe you should. Maybe that's better anyway."

Pickett's leash was coiled on the floor. Lenore gathered it up and clipped it to his collar and opened the passenger-side door and followed Pickett out. Mr. Bishop and Coach Fink went quiet, as if just now recalling her presence. Pickett relieved himself in the weeds, then started down the shoulder like he knew where he was going. Lenore let him tug her along. It was her fault they were in this mess. After a few seconds Mr. Bishop trotted up beside her, and a few seconds after that Coach Fink caught up as well, matching Pickett's pace along the road.

"I thought you were waiting with the car," Mr. Bishop said.

"I changed my mind."

"Did you lock the doors?"

"You think somebody's gonna steal that car?" Coach Fink said. "It'd be your lucky day if somebody stole that hunk of turd."

They'd been walking for maybe fifteen minutes, Pickett in the lead, his nose close to the ground as if tracking some specific scent, when the country store came into view around a bend in the road, sign rising from a gravel parking lot, the lot washed nearly clear of actual gravel by who knows how many rains, leaving packed earth and potholes and battered railroad ties marking the spots. Mother's Best. The letters as weathered as the porch planks. A solitary car out front, a blue Mercedes with a broken taillight.

Mr. Bishop and Coach Fink stopped abruptly side by side.

"Somebody's yanking my chain," Coach Fink said.

Lenore was holding Pickett's leash, and he dragged her a few steps more before she was able to bring him to a halt. "What is it?"

Mr. Bishop said, "That's her car," and just then the door of Mother's Best swung open and Eugenia Marsh stepped out, a brown-paper shopping bag cradled in her arms. Lenore recognized her right away. From that distance she hardly seemed to have aged since her Briarwood days. Eugenia Marsh noticed them and smiled.

"You don't mean to tell me that you walked all this way? It's true that I receive the occasional pilgrim but never anything so extreme."

Mr. Bishop pointed back the way they'd come. "My car broke down."

Eugenia Marsh set the bag on the roof of her Mercedes and crossed the parking lot in their direction. She extended a hand to Lenore.

"You must be Jenny March," she said.

Given the circumstances—Mr. Bishop's car breaking down, Eugenia Marsh's sudden appearance, the effect of those developments compounded by everything that had happened in the past few months, including but not limited to her recent conversations with the ghost of Elizabeth Archer—she might have been forgiven for forgetting her real name, but she managed to blurt it out after a second.

"How alliterative," said Eugenia Marsh. She flicked a hand at the paper bag. "I came for snacks. I don't generally keep snacks in the house, certainly not the sort of snacks a teenager might enjoy."

"You were expecting us?" Coach Fink said, and Eugenia Marsh said, "I had a dream last night," as if that explained anything at all.

Pickett whined and darted his gaze from face to face. He sat suddenly, as if commanded, then stood up again. He gave his tail a tentative wag. Lenore knew how he felt. She passed the leash to Mr. Bishop.

"Here's an idea," said Eugenia Marsh. "Why don't Lenore and I adjourn to my house, while you two ring for a tow? Try Toby Giles. He's in the book. He's kept my Mercedes running far beyond the span of its natural life. Once you've squared everything away, you can join us. Toby will be happy to give you a lift."

Mr. Bishop said, "I don't think that's a good idea."

"Don't be silly. I appreciate your concern, but you know I'm harmless, and besides, your car needs repairing, and Lenore and I require time alone." She looked at Lenore, her eyes excited. "That's why you came, isn't it, dear?"

"I guess," Lenore said, still a little dazed, but despite the uncertainty in her reply, she understood that this was, in fact, precisely why she'd come. A private audience with Eugenia Marsh. That's what she'd wanted all along. Mr. Bishop and Coach Fink would only be in the way. "It's all right, Mr. Bishop."

Eugenia Marsh said, "Of course it is." She was already steering Lenore toward her Mercedes, one hand on the small of her back. "Tell me—what brand of soda do you prefer? I wasn't sure, so I bought Coke, 7-Up, and Mountain Dew."

"Coke is fine," Lenore said.

"And Doritos—how do you feel about Doritos?"

"I like Doritos," Lenore said.

"You wait one damn minute," Coach Fink said. "You're not leaving here with that girl."

In no hurry, Eugenia Marsh lifted the shopping bag down from the roof of her car, opened the trunk, and set the bag inside. "As I recall," she said, "it was a dream that brought you to me in the first place. Isn't that right? Doesn't it follow that a dream should herald your return?"

To Lenore's surprise, Coach Fink failed to respond, and Mr. Bishop just stood there, holding Pickett's leash. Lenore hardly registered lowering herself into the passenger seat. Even before starting the car, Eugenia Marsh began to describe her dream. "So I was a girl," she said, "and I was back at Briarwood," and off they went, Mr. Bishop and Coach Fink and Pickett receding in the rear windshield until they were small enough that Lenore could have held them in the palm of her hand.

XXII

She was a girl again, and she was back at Briarwood, and night had fallen over campus, and she was walking all alone across the quad and could hear a baby crying somewhere in the dark. Such an obvious symbol. Even dreaming, part of her was aware of the heavy-handedness of her subconscious, but in no way did this awareness render the sound any less desperate, any less heart-wrenching. She searched for the baby in Everett Hall and Blackford Hall without success. She searched the library and chapel, each building thick with shadows, her footsteps echoing, not another soul to be found. Sometimes the crying grew louder as she searched, and she was sure that she would come upon the baby in the next room, around the next corner, but the sound would fade and she understood that she had been searching the wrong building altogether. And then she was running up the hill toward Thornton Hall—it seemed impossibly far away—and even though her conscious mind informed her sleeping mind that all of this was just a dream, that there was no baby, that she was right here in her bed, her heart was pounding in her physical body and the body in her dream, and she couldn't catch her breath, and she knew that if she failed to find the baby soon, something terrible would happen, something final.

"It's so embarrassing," she said, reaching up to touch her cheek. "At my age. I'd like to believe that after all this time, I was capable of a more original dream."

"I'm not following," the girl said. "How did you know we were coming?"

"Let me finish," she said, and she described how she burst into Thornton Hall, and right away she could hear the baby's cries bleating down from the second floor. She took the stairs two at a time, the crying suddenly all around her, the way the sound of the ocean fills your ears when you're underwater, holding your breath, your heart thump-thump-thumping inside your head. Now she realized where the sound had been leading her all along. "My old room," she told the girl. "Room 208. Elizabeth's room." She raced down the hall and pushed open the door, and instantly the crying stopped. "And there I was," she said, with a flourish in her voice, and even as she steered her old Mercedes past the mailbox and down the drive, she felt that rush of recognition all over again, her waking self and her dream self washed with comprehension and relief, a feeling like landing on the right line of dialogue in one of her plays, a certainty beyond reason but no less palpable and true.

"And there you were?" the girl said as Eugenia parked the car beside the house.

"There I was," Eugenia said.

She dropped her hands into her lap and regarded this girl in her car—this Lenore Littlefield, this Jenny March.

"I used to live in 208," the girl said.

"I assumed as much," Eugenia said, delighted. "So now you see?"

"See what?"

Eugenia pressed her lips together, tried again. "I met myself. In my old room. I met Jenny March. I met *you*."

She performed another flourish with her voice to emphasize the last word, but the light refused to flicker on behind the girl's eyes.

"Where was the baby?" the girl said.

"There was no baby, not a literal one."

The girl said, "I'm confused."

Eugenia looked away. The sun streamed down. It was beginning to feel a little close inside the car. Very well then. If she had to spell it out for this girl, then that's what she would do.

"You were pregnant, were you not?"

"How did you know that?"

"Your teacher told me."

"Mr. Bishop—why? He shouldn't have told you that. That's private. He had no business telling you."

"Well, he did. He believed it was important for me to know, and he was right. But surely now you understand."

The girl blinked half a dozen times in quick succession. None of this was transpiring the way Eugenia had imagined.

"I'm sorry," the girl said. "This is—I don't know—it's a lot. Not just you. Everything. The last few months. I'm sorry."

Eugenia sighed. Three decades had slipped away since her time at Briarwood. She touched the girl's elbow with her fingertips.

"Let's see about those snacks," she said.

Eugenia had spent the morning cleaning house. Amazing the mess a solitary person can make. You would think the opposite would be true—the more people, the greater the mess. It's the peripheral details of tidiness that escape one's attention living alone. Eugenia made her bed each day and hung her towel on its rack after a bath. She did not let dishes pile up in the sink or dirty clothes accumulate in the laundry hamper. She managed quite capably the daily clutter of her life. All the while, however, over all these sequestered years, cobwebs had spun into being in every corner of the ceiling, and dust had been silting down on the mantel and the windowsills, on baseboards and the tops of picture frames. Unnoticed, mildew propagated in the seams of bathroom tile. She'd swung out of bed that morning, invigorated by her dream, and immediately she began to clean. She told herself that even if the dream proved to be a dud, at least the house would be in order and she wouldn't have to broom cobwebs from the ceiling or scrub baseboards for years and years. Three hours later her enthusiasm had diminished slightly, worn down by the scope of the task, but the house was gleaming, and she opened the refrigerator to pour herself a celebratory glass of milk. The milk was right where she'd left it, but mostly what she'd noticed was all the empty space. There was butter in the little compartment, lettuce and carrots in the crisper, soy sauce and Dijon mustard and a half-empty bottle of sauvignon blanc on the door. And that, more or less, was all. She could hardly entertain a teenage girl with these supplies, so off she rushed to Mother's Best. She would rather have driven to the supermarket in Lexington, but the day was already getting on and she worried she might miss the girl if she was gone too long, but even in this instance the forces of the universe were at work, delivering the girl directly to her, or her to the girl, depending on your point of view, delivering each to the other, as forecast by her dream.

"It is a proven scientific fact," she explained to Lenore, "that energy is neither created nor destroyed. You know this. I have no idea who is teaching in the sciences at Briarwood anymore—surely Mr. Reese is long dead—but I'm certain that whoever they are they have not failed to mention the first law of thermodynamics." Lenore nodded and sipped her Coke. For her part, Eugenia had been intrigued by the radiator-fluid tint of the Mountain Dew. They were seated on opposite sides of the breakfast table, a mid-century piece with aluminum legs that had survived her New York days, a bowl of Doritos between them. "If this is true of tangible things—the wood which becomes the fire which becomes the smoke—it must also be true of the intangible as well."

"Are you talking about ghosts?" Lenore said.

"That's just one example," Eugenia said. "Our thoughts, our dreams, the very force that beats our hearts. What else is existence except another form of energy? If we follow this line of thinking, it might be argued that all existence has been recurring in one form or another since the beginning of time."

"History repeats itself?" Lenore said, and now the light really did blink on behind her eyes as visibly as if someone had thrown a switch.

"Indeed," Eugenia said, "but these energies are much more inscrutable than such a literal phrase implies. Empires inevitably fall, frequently for similar reasons, but they never fall in precisely the same way. There is always an element of the particular in their demise."

Lenore drew in a long breath, the sort of breath that often precedes a question of considerable gravity, but she released it without speaking. She reached for the bowl but withdrew her hand without taking a Dorito. She glanced at Eugenia, then dropped her eyes. Finally, she folded her hands one atop the other on the table.

So Eugenia answered the question she knew Lenore had been suppressing all this time. "In the winter of my junior year at Briarwood," she said, "I met a boy during a production of *The Seagull* by Anton Chekhov. He was playing Trigorin. I'd been cast as Nina."

"What was his name?" Lenore said.

"His name is unimportant."

Lenore raised her eyes.

"His name was Cortland Teasdale," Eugenia said, "but everyone called him Cort. He went to Woodmont. He was a senior. He had brown hair and brown eyes, and he smelled like rain and cigarette smoke." She paused a moment to assess the effect of these details. "Satisfied?"

Lenore nodded and took a chip.

"Thank heavens, because that's about all I can remember."

This wasn't true—she could recall almost everything about him, from the cowlick at the back of his head to the fact that he kept dimes in his loafers instead of pennies—but she did believe that the minutiae were beside the point. She suspected that she would have kissed most any Woodmont boy backstage, provided that he was moderately handsome and displayed at least a modicum of talent. She would have taken him by the hand, whoever he might have been, and slipped away from the cast party and sneaked him up the back stairs to her room, not only because the play itself had cast a spell but because that was just about the worst thing a Briarwood girl could do, and to her younger self the worst thing always seemed so much more vital, so much more interesting than the best. Sneaking a boy into your room wasn't even all that dangerous and rare. She knew dozens of older girls who claimed to have gotten away with it. What were the odds that her RA would walk in on them while Eugenia was buttoning her blouse, Cortland Teasdale lingering in her bed, still astounded at his good fortune? What were the chances that this single assignation would leave her pregnant, a fact she wouldn't discover until after she had been suspended from Briarwood and she woke one morning in her parents' house sick to her stomach for no good reason? Or that her father would be so averse to one scandal that he was willing to risk another? Or that her mother would know exactly which unscrupulous doctor to call? Or that her rebellious younger self would turn out to be so weak-willed, so staggered and heartsick, that she would go along with every single thing that happened without protest or complaint? The odds, it turned out, were very good, though her younger self couldn't have known that larger energies were at play, energies that would one day deliver Lenore Littlefield to her kitchen table.

"So Elizabeth didn't come to you until—after?" Lenore said, letting that word, *after*, stand in for all that it implied.

"That's right. After. I changed the details in the play. The conflict is more immediate if the decision hasn't already been made."

"By why did she come to you?"

"You already know," Eugenia said.

"She was pregnant," Lenore said. "She was pregnant when she died."

"She never said as much. She didn't like to talk about her suicide. But I don't think we're off the mark."

"Why didn't you put that in the play?"

Before Eugenia could reply, there came a slapping sound from the next room, and Lenore startled in her chair.

"That'll be a bird," Eugenia said. "The poor things fly into the windows. The windows reflect the sky over the fields this time of day."

Very slowly, like a pantomime, Lenore brought her hands up from the table and covered her eyes. Crying. Her shoulders trembled but she hardly made a sound. Eugenia sipped her Mountain Dew while she waited. Finally, Lenore lowered her hands, and as she did, someone knocked on the door, three sharp raps, her coach and her teacher returning to claim their charge. Eugenia stood and rested a palm on Lenore's shoulder.

"Just because it's not directly addressed," she said, "doesn't mean it's not in the play."

Question 6

On September 28, 1994, Disney CEO Michael Eisner announced the termination of the Disney's America project, later claiming in various interviews that its failure was the "greatest disappointment" of his executive tenure. Which of the following is/are believed to be responsible for dooming the historical theme park to cancellation?

A) Financial concerns related to the project, including a 40 percent increase in the estimated cost of construction.

B) Legislative efforts funded by local landowners and spearheaded by organizations such as the Piedmont Environmental Council and National Trust for Historic Preservation.

C) A shift in public perception steered in large part by a group of notable historians and celebrities and writers, among them Eugenia Marsh, who purchased a full-page ad in the *Washington Post* referring to Michael Eisner as "the man who would destroy American history."

D) All of the above.

XXIII

Lenore lay in bed in the dark waiting for the phone to ring. Sunday night. Then Monday, Tuesday. Her ears became fine-tuned to every tick and shuffle and mutter in Thornton Hall. Why would Elizabeth abandon her just now? She must have dozed, she told herself, but it didn't feel that way. Strangely, those long nights did not leave her ragged with exhaustion. She felt a little dreamy in class but also perceptive and alive, alert to something just beyond her reach.

On Wednesday, Coach Fink kept the cast late to rehearse the scene in which Eleanor's ghost compares memory to dreaming, Jenny's loneliness and confusion getting the better of her fear. Afterward, Juliet caught up to Lenore on her way down to the dining hall.

"I'm already so nervous I could puke," she said.

A curious alteration had occurred in Juliet. She had, it seemed, absorbed Eugenia Marsh's advice on some fundamental level, her Eleanor Bowman so restrained these last two weeks as to be downright otherworldly.

"It'll be great," Lenore said. "You'll be great."

Her parents planned to attend. All of them. She hadn't wanted them to find out, but Willow had spotted a notice in the school newsletter and called Lenore's mom, who called Lenore acting all indignant that Lenore hadn't told her, when really she was pissed that Willow had found out first. Now flights had been booked, hotel rooms reserved.

"Do you think she'll come?" Juliet said.

The question was briefly disorienting for Lenore—was she referring to her mom or Willow, and why did she care?—but then she realized that Juliet was asking about Eugenia Marsh. Debate about her presence or lack thereof had dominated discussion before and after rehearsal ever since Coach Fink made her announcement. As for Lenore, she had her doubts. And though she could imagine a perverse pleasure in dashing Juliet's hopes, she didn't see the point. How hard would it be to keep one more secret?

"Shit," she said, smacking her forehead. "I left my backpack."

This was, in fact, the case. Lenore was suddenly aware of the absence of the backpack's weight on her shoulders. She wasn't sure if her forgetfulness was a result of lack of sleep or post-rehearsal abstraction, but she trotted back up the hill toward the auditorium, picturing her backpack right where she'd left it, on a chair in the second row, three seats from the aisle. She rarely went anywhere on campus without her backpack. Lenore banged into the lobby and stopped, her attention arrested by an unexpected sound—singing. A lone voice, sturdy and clear. "Tonight, tonight, won't be just any night." Lenore crept across the carpet and peeked into the auditorium. Coach Fink was standing between the beds onstage, bathed in a solitary spotlight. "Tonight, there'll be no morning star." Her eyes were closed, her chin tipped toward the back row, her shadow puddled at her feet. Lenore was reminded of those images of Coach Fink in the yearbook. She could see her backpack exactly where she'd thought it would be, but she made no move to retrieve it. The dust rising in the spotlight and Coach Fink's voice rising with it filled Lenore with anticipation—any moment now and something important might occur. Something might be understood.

But nothing happened. No signal descended from the universe, no message was received. Half a minute ticked by, and then the last words of the song were fading on the air, and Coach Fink slipped backstage to shut off the lights. Lenore took advantage of her absence to scurry down the aisle and nab her backpack and beat it out of the auditorium undetected.

Her mother was the first to arrive, consolation for being the last to know. She flew into Dulles on Thursday morning, rented a car, and drove directly to campus to sign Lenore out for lunch. They ate in Manassas because none of the restaurants in Haymarket was good enough, but even in Manassas the pickings were pretty slim. Her mother recalled a sandwich shop, a favorite of Briarwood parents for its tablecloths and chicken salad.

"How on earth," she said to Lenore, "did you ever wind up in a play?"

"I was curious, I guess. I didn't think I'd get the lead."

This didn't feel like a lie. She wasn't concealing the fact that Drama Club had been a punishment for missing curfew so much as she was committing to a role. For the duration of this meal, she would be performing the part of Lenore Littlefield. She never felt like herself around her mother anyway. She was always impersonating her mother's idea of her. The sandwich shop consisted of eight tables in the front room of what had once been someone's house—handwritten menu on a chalkboard, display case filled with baked goods. The proprietress came and went, timing iced tea refills so as not to interrupt the scene.

In American Lit they'd been discussing *The Phantom of Thornton Hall* all week, and Ms. Pinn was finally ready to hash out the ending—what did it mean that the stage went black with Jenny at the window, so many questions left unanswered?

"I think it's about suicide," said Grace LaPointe, who hadn't cared about literature before the riding instructor took over but had morphed into a first-rate kiss-ass ever since.

Ms. Pinn nodded and touched her throat.

"Interesting," she said. "Go on, Grace."

"Well, why else would it end like that? She's pregnant. She's young. She has no good choices. The ghost hasn't helped. What else can she do? Plus, Eleanor's suicide foreshadows Jenny's."

These discussions made Lenore self-conscious, not only because she was playing Jenny March but because Ms. Pinn often goaded her to participate, as if Lenore possessed some special knowledge.

"Miss Littlefield," she said, "what do you think?"

"It's not about suicide," Lenore said.

Ms. Pinn straddled a chair and crossed her arms over the seat back.

"What then? Tell us."

"It's meant to be thrilling," Lenore said. "Anything could happen next."

She didn't hear the bell so much as react to it, rising, stowing her notebook, the current of girls washing her out into the light. She had felt so close to understanding at Eugenia Marsh's house. Of course, the woman's theories had seemed ridiculous, but they'd also made a kind of sense that afternoon, the way algebra could seem perfectly logical in class but fade to mystery when Lenore sat down to do her homework.

Melissa turned and smiled and walked backward a few steps.

"You coming?" she said, and Lenore felt her insides lift.

They were only running up to a convenience store for Slushees and M&M's but Melissa drove with the windows down, an R.E.M. tape in the deck. They took the long way back to campus. Past the water tower and over the railroad tracks. They had to shout over the wind and the music, their tongues gone Slushee blue, woods pressing in on both sides, and they had no idea that they were skirting the edges of the Disney site, no idea that the project would fall apart over the next few months or that the trees blurring past would remain undisturbed for years, until a new set of developers bought up the land and razed everything for a golf course, lining the links with many-windowed homes, or that those same developers would purchase Briarwood not too many years after that, converting the school into an assisted-living facility for well-heeled retirees. How could they have known? They could hardly see beyond the next bend and then the long straightaway to campus, blacktop tapering into nothing beyond the gates.

Coach Fink was all business at dress rehearsal. She walked them calmly through each scene. No surprise to Lenore. Her coach was always coiled within herself on the eve of a big game. "I want you strong. I want you at your best. Get a good night's sleep," she said, but sleep gusted out ahead of Lenore like an autumn leaf in the wind. Light moved across the ceiling, footsteps moved on the second floor. Melissa was curled up with her back to Lenore, quilt drawn to her ears.

Lenore thought about energy, the universe. She thought about history—did it mean anything to her beyond tests and papers and places and dates? Did it matter that Jefferson Davis was the president of the Confederacy or that those people in Selma had marched with such dignity across the Edmund Pettus Bridge? Those facts had no immediate bearing on her life. But even then, sleep receding by the minute, she sensed that she was mistaken, that somewhere beyond the grasp of her conscious mind lay another answer altogether, one that accounted for Disney and trench warfare and premonitory dreams and the atom bomb and ghosts and her role as Jenny March. She also sensed that this answer would elude her for the rest of her life, no matter how many hours of sleep she lost in its pursuit.

She sighed and swung her legs around and tiptoed down the hall. She ducked into the phone closet. Shut the door behind her. She hit the light switch and found Nate's number on the wall. Instead, she called Domino's Pizza—closed for the night—and J. Crew customer service. "Hello?" the operator said. "How can I help you? Would you like to place an order? Hello?" She tried the number that would tell you the time in Mobile, Alabama. 12:08 a.m. An hour earlier down there. The woman on the recording had a Southern accent, a real one, rich and slow. The light in the common room blinked on and off again. Had someone said her name? Lenore stepped out, holding her breath.

"Who's there?" she whispered, and a voice said, "Boo," and Lenore jumped, whirling toward the sound. She sat down hard and clapped a hand over her mouth to keep from calling out.

"It's me," the voice said. "It's just me," and Lenore recognized Poppy hovering over her.

"Jesus Christ, Poppy. What are you doing here?"

Poppy laughed, pleased with the effect of her surprise. "Melissa let me in through the window. I came to see you in the play." She lowered herself beside Lenore and gave her a clumsy, one-armed hug. "I took the bus," she said. "I left the best note. It says I've run away with the neighbor's pool boy. That'll buy me a little time. The bus, in case you were wondering, could not have been any more repellent."

Lenore shot an elbow into Poppy's ribs. "But they won't let you come back to Briarwood. Not after this. Your parents won't let you come back next year."

"I'm not sure I want to come back," Poppy said. "I've been thinking I want to check out public school. Fret over my outfit every morning. Date a boy who drives a crappy car. I want to live in the real world for a while."

"That is the dumbest thing I've ever heard you say."

"What?"

"You have to come back."

"Briarwood's just so weird. It's all bullshit."

In another few minutes, they would adjourn to what had been Poppy's room and stay up talking with Melissa until daylight revealed itself against the windows, but for now neither of them moved. All around them Thornton Hall was quiet, the particular and restless silence of a hundred girls asleep. Lenore would have sworn she felt a presence in the dark.

"But it's ours," she said.

In the morning, not long before the first bell rang, Valerie Beech unlocked the doors to the Herndon Annex, Connie Booth brought the chandeliers to life in Ransom Library. On the front porch of Briarwood Manor, Linwood Mackey offered his wife a puff of his cigar. After a while, the bell tolled in the quad, ringing in what was, for the majority of students, an ordinary Friday. Most of the girls planned to attend the play, but not all. Grace LaPointe and her stallion, Tabasco, would be competing in a horse show over the weekend, and Marisol Brooks refused to go on principle. What could be more pitiful, she wanted to know, than student theater? Besides, there was no rush. There would be a matinee tomorrow.

But first—an Art History quiz, a Cicero translation, a softball game, the Briarwood Vixens versus the Lady Cardinals of Saint Mary's, the plink of an aluminum bat carrying all the way to Faculty Row. There were girls lounging on the library steps, others reading on the benches in the quad, another bunch painting some kind of banner in the grass, squirrels leaping from branch to branch above them, making the leaves rustle and shimmer, the scene like a photograph from one of Briarwood's brochures.

And that evening, while the cast made jittery, last-minute preparations backstage, cars wound past the gatehouse and along Shady Dell Loop to the parking lot beside Terrell Field. At Bishop's suggestion, the grounds crew had lined a path with candles, threads of smoke ghosting up from small white paper bags. Great sprays of daffodils and hydrangeas waited just inside the doors. Freshmen in Briarwood dress blazers greeted arriving audience members and presented them with programs. More freshmen ushered them to their seats. Headmistress Mackey roamed the lobby, hailing parents she recognized, lavishing special attention on those who might be interested in her new computer lab. No sign of Eugenia Marsh. Headmistress Mackey was beginning to let herself believe that her plan had worked and opening night could proceed without undo complication.

Bishop, too, had been wondering about the guest of honor. As he stood between the open double doors and scanned the audience, chatter filling the air, he couldn't make her out in the crowd and, to his surprise, he felt relieved. Decked out in green-and-white bunting, washed with decorous light, the auditorium looked dressed and ready for a momentous occasion. He thought of Coach Fink, pacing and fuming backstage. Without discussing the matter, they had arrived at a kind of truce. They would return to mutual disregard. When their paths crossed on campus, they might exchange a nod, an offhand smile, but nothing more. This, too, made him relieved and also grateful and also sad from time to time, though he understood that history, personal or otherwise, cannot be expunged.

At precisely seven o'clock, while Coach Fink was rounding up the cast behind the curtain, Headmistress Mackey commenced her dedication at a lectern on the apron of the stage.

"In the last one hundred and twenty-six years, Briarwood School for Girls has produced some of the most outstanding women in America. I don't have to name for this audience all the remarkable young ladies who have passed through our halls. It is precisely because we settle for nothing less that we run the risk of taking that tradition of excellence for granted."

"Everybody get in here," Coach Fink said. "Bring it in."

"There are times, however, when an alumna's achievements are so extraordinary that they demand permanent commemoration so that future students will be reminded of what is possible when a young woman builds her dreams on the foundation laid at this school."

Coach Fink extended her hand, fingers spread, palm down.

"Eugenia Marsh matriculated at Briarwood in 1958, on the eve of one of the most tumultuous decades in our nation's history. She was a dedicated member of the Drama Club and participated in numerous productions on this very stage. After graduation, she built on her Briarwood experience to compose an enduring work of American theater. *The Phantom of Thornton Hall* received the Pulitzer Prize for Drama in 1974, and Miss Marsh's words have been translated into thirteen languages and performed by some of the most talented actors in the world. We'd hoped Miss Marsh could be with us here tonight, but she's given enough already to us all."

The girls pushed in tight and piled their hands atop Coach Fink's.

"Ladies and gentlemen, I present to you the Eugenia Marsh Stage in the Beatrix Garvey Memorial Auditorium."

As a pair of ushers peeled away the bunting along the lip of the stage to reveal a commemorative brass plaque, Coach Fink said, "So she's a no-show. Hell with her. Whatever happens out there tonight belongs to you, not her. Let's make history, ladies. 'Drama Club' on three. One, two, three."

Their hands leaped up with their voices, their voices muffled by applause. The house lights flickered, and Headmistress Mackey made her exit, and the girls hurried to their places. Lenore arranged herself in the bed in her white nightgown and closed her eyes. It seemed possible in that moment that she might actually fall asleep, that she might wake to another life. Already, she could feel herself dissolving, becoming, the moment spooling out and out and out, whispers fading in the crowd, then a pulse of perfect silence before the curtain opened on a dorm room at a boarding school not so different from Briarwood School for Girls.

Question 7

The March 31, 1994, edition of the *Thorn* was dominated almost entirely by news of *The Phantom of Thornton Hall*. Including the review, there were three full articles and a sidebar. Which of the following items rated the front page?

A) Praise for Lenore Littlefield's performance as Jenny March, which the staff critic called "unsettling" and "entirely authentic" and "quietly heartbreaking."

B) The dedication of the stage to Eugenia Marsh during a ceremony presided over by Headmistress Mackey, who was quoted as saying, among other things, "Let Ms. Marsh's achievement stand as an inspiration to Briarwood students everywhere."

C) Several unconfirmed sightings of Eugenia Marsh, who, according to one of the freshman ushers, "slipped in late, just as the lights were going down," and was seen, according to another, "on her feet at the end, bawling her eyes out," though there were numerous inconsistencies in these reports, and none of them could be substantiated.

D) A disturbance during the curtain call in which a suspended student, Poppy Tuttle, wearing a ski mask and Mickey Mouse ears, charged onto the apron of the stage, shouting, "Down with Disney" and "Long Live the Red Hand" and "Sic Semper Tyrannis" before hurling a water balloon at Headmistress Mackey, who was seated in the front row.

Acknowledgments

At Briarwood School for Girls is set at a fictional boarding school in Prince William County, Virginia, its action largely confined to dorm rooms and classrooms and field trips and so on, its principal focus the individual dramas of a handful of students and teachers, coaches and administrators, but hovering around the periphery of these more personal stories is Disney's very real attempt to build a historical theme park in the area. I have allowed myself a measure of artistic license in portraying these events (the Disney representative, for example, who appears in these pages is entirely a creature of my imagination), but I have also made an effort to hew as closely as possible to the facts, including, in some instances, echoing the language of press releases and promotional brochures issued by Disney at the time. Especially useful in my research were Michael Eisner's memoir, *Work in Progress*; the website micechat.com; and coverage of the controversy by the *Washington Post*.

This book would not exist at all without my godfather, Stillman Knight, who reminded me of the Disney's America project over dinner some years back and stirred up my interest in the subject. Thank you, Stilly, for the idea and for picking up the tab.

Thanks to Jenny Long, a former Virginia boarding school girl herself, who told me via email about a button she once acquired at a horse race in Middleburg, Virginia. Her story could not have arrived at a more opportune moment in revision and her button appears now in these pages.

Many thanks to my agent, Warren Frazier, whose belief in this book has been unflagging from the start; and to my editor, Elisabeth Schmitz, for her patience and her savvy as a reader. Thanks, as well, to Morgan Entrekin and Deb Seager and Katie Raissian and Jazmine Goguen and every single human at Grove Atlantic for their support over the years.

More thanks to James McLaughlin, who read the very first draft of this novel and the very last; and to Beth Ann Fennelly, Tom Franklin, Shannon Burke, Susan Pepper Robbins, Elizabeth Weld, and Margaret Lazarus Dean, all of whom read versions of this novel along the way and each of whom made it better.

Thanks to my wife, Jill, for her beautiful cover; and to my daughters, Mary and Helen, who have taught me so much about what it means to be a fine young woman.

Thanks to my colleagues and students at the University of Tennessee.

And thank you, finally, to the state of Virginia, where I lived for a number of years, first as a student at Hampden-Sydney College and the University of Virginia and then as a Visiting Writer at Hollins University. Virginia strikes me as unusually rich in single gender institutions, several of which provided inspiration for elements of this novel. I hope this book does justice to my fond memories of the years that I called Virginia home.